"I have a question, Judge McBride."

"Yes, Mr. O'Malley?"

"Would you have dinner with me tonight?"

Becky blinked. Surely she hadn't heard him correctly. "Excuse me?" she said, and tried to ignore the warm flush climbing up her chest.

"I asked if you'd go out with me tonight."

The court audience leaned forward, eagerly anticipating her response.

Will O'Malley was, without a doubt, the best-looking defendant who'd ever stood before her. The fact that he'd pleaded guilty straight up—rather than offer a host of excuses—impressed her. But he *was* a defendant and strictly off-limits.

Furious that her body was telling her one thing, while her brain told her another, Becky answered him more harshly than she'd intended. "No, Mr. O'Malley, I won't," she said and slammed down her gavel. "Get [illegible] of my court!"

Dear Reader,

This is my debut novel for Harlequin American Romance. I loved creating this "opposites attract" story about an unconventional hero, Will O'Malley, who is hauled into court by his law-abiding brother. Will takes one look at the judge and decides he's going to marry her. So begins his tale of winning straitlaced judge Becky McBride's love.

Will's story started many years earlier when I was writing his brother Matt's romance. I learned that Sheriff Matt had brothers—four of them—and the one who was most insistent about having his story told was Will. But Will's story wasn't so easy to create. He was an unconventional hero who needed a lot of taming! I detail his journey to winning Becky's heart—and this book's journey to publication—in a research paper that you can read, if you wish, on my Web site, www.cccoburn.com. I hope it will help provide a guide to unpublished authors.

As you can see from the cover, *Colorado Christmas* is part of THE O'MALLEY MEN miniseries, so watch for Will's other brothers' stories of finding love in the mountain town of Spruce Lake.

Happy reading! Healthy lives! And a Merry Christmas to all!

Love,

C.C. Coburn

Colorado Christmas

C.C. COBURN

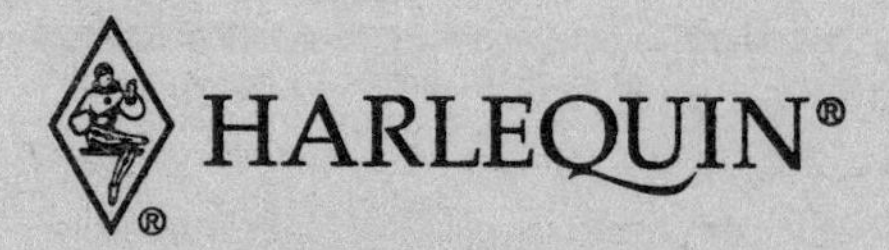

TORONTO • NEW YORK • LONDON
AMSTERDAM • PARIS • SYDNEY • HAMBURG
STOCKHOLM • ATHENS • TOKYO • MILAN • MADRID
PRAGUE • WARSAW • BUDAPEST • AUCKLAND

ISBN-13: 978-0-373-75287-4

COLORADO CHRISTMAS

This edition published by arrangement with Harlequin Books S.A.

www.eHarlequin.com

Printed in U.S.A.

ABOUT THE AUTHOR

C.C. Coburn married the first man who asked her and hasn't regretted a day since—well, not many of them! She grew up in Australia's outback, moved to its sun-drenched Pacific coast, then traveled the world. A keen skier, she discovered Colorado's majestic Rocky Mountains and now divides her time between Australia and Colorado. Home will always be Australia, where she lives with her husband, three grown children, a Labrador and three cats—but her heart and soul are also firmly planted in Colorado. When she isn't writing or skiing, C.C. loves to sculpt, paint, surf and play with her Lab. She loves hearing from readers. You can visit her at www.cccoburn.com.

Acknowledgments

I would like to thank the members of Romance Writers of Australia; my wonderful critique partner, Kelly Hunter; the members of my local Romance Writers Support group: Helen Bianchin, Noela Cowell, Louise Cusack, Helen Lacey and Lesley Millar and my Masters in Writing cohort: Sandra Barletta, Lisa Barry, Marilyn Carey, Louise Ousby, Melynda Genrich and our supervisor, Dr. Glen Thomas.

I received invaluable insights into law enforcement in Colorado and offer my heartfelt thanks to Summit County Judge Ed Casias and Captain Erik Bourgerie and Deputy Ron Hochmuth of the Summit County Sheriff's Office—who gave me a most interesting tour of the County jail—and Craig Simson of Keystone Ski Patrol for his help with avalanche rescue.

I would especially like to thank my editor, Paula Eykelhof, to whom I (badly) pitched this story, but who managed to see its potential and supported me through two long years to publication. I value our friendship forged through this journey and am deeply indebted to her faith in me.

My children, Catherine, Holly and Jock, without whom this book would have been finished many years earlier.

And last, my husband and best friend, Keith, who has always been my greatest supporter and fan, even though he's never read a word I've written.

Chapter One

Will O'Malley stomped the snow from his boots before entering the courthouse in Spruce Lake, Colorado.

His brother Matt collared him as he stepped inside. "Where the *hell* have you been?"

Will grinned at his arresting officer, unfazed by his angry demand. "Delivering flowers for Mrs. C."

Matt could be such a stuffed shirt sometimes—so could his other three brothers—but Matt was the one who worried most about what people thought of the O'Malleys. To make amends, he caught Matt in a bear hug. "Thanks for coming along to support me, buddy."

Matt shrugged him off, saying through clenched teeth, "I'm not here to *support* you. I'm here to make sure you don't get in any more trouble." He led the way into the courtroom, then spun around. "You're aware that I might run for county sheriff, aren't you? Your antics last night won't help my chances."

Will doubted the residents of Peaks County thought any less of Matt or the rest of the O'Malleys after last night, considering most of the courtroom audience—Will noted with pleasure—were with him at the time. "Sure. In fact, I'll be your campaign manager."

"Over my dead body," Matt growled as Will stepped up to the podium and turned toward the bench.

Wow! was his first reaction as he studied the judge. Her dark red hair was pulled back in a severe style that went with her suit and gavel. A few tendrils had worked themselves loose, softening her face and contrasting with her otherwise flawless presentation. She looked serious in a strangely attractive way and would probably send him to the slammer, if she could guess his thoughts. She looked up, trained her green eyes on Will and he felt something hit him deep in his gut.

Every year at their wedding anniversary party, Mac O'Malley told the story of how he vowed he'd marry their mother, Sarah, the moment he laid eyes on her. Until now, Will had believed that was just Irish blarney.

Convinced he was gazing at the woman he'd marry and needing to share his feelings with Matt, he murmured, "I'm going to marry that woman someday."

JUDGE REBECCA MCBRIDE had finished her previous case concerning a pig called Louella who'd run amok in a dress boutique. Feeling as though she was caught up in reruns of *Green Acres,* she wondered yet again, *Why on earth did I take this job?*

Steeling herself, she glanced up, ready to face the next bizarre case. Her eyes locked with the defendant's and her heart rate kicked up several notches.

Who knew this town of four ski mountains, three sets of traffic lights, 2,597 residents and one extremely naughty pig had some attractions, after all?

"Shut up!" Deputy O'Malley hissed.

Becky peered over the top of her glasses. "Were you speaking to me?"

"No, Judge. I was speaking to my—" he glared at the defendant "*—brother.*"

That would explain the striking similarity. However, Deputy O'Malley was, as always, dressed immaculately, while his brother wore faded blue jeans, tan cowboy boots and a chambray shirt that stretched across broad shoulders. His neatly pressed shirt was at odds with his too-long black hair.

"The defendant is my *younger* brother, Judge. Any resemblance ends with our appearance," the deputy said.

She clasped her hands in front of her, steepled her thumbs and gave the defendant her most intimidating stare. "Mr. O'Malley, you've been charged with damaging demolition equipment belonging to the Mountain Resorts Development Company. How do you plead?"

"Guilty, Your Honor."

His admission surprised her. So did her own response to his deep-dimpled smile. It went clear up to his dark brown eyes and did inexplicable things to her insides.

She took a deep, calming breath before saying, "Why did you vandalize the vehicles?"

"The company has bought an entire block at the north end of Main Street. They want to demolish the existing buildings in order to erect an eight-story condominium complex and shopping mall," he explained.

"Those buildings are derelict. I should think a shopping mall and housing—given the town's shortage—would rejuvenate the area," Becky pointed out.

"Granted. But they're fine examples of Colorado Victorian architecture. Although many haven't been occupied since the gold mines closed back in '49, with sensitive renovation they could be restored to their former glory."

Becky admired his passion, if not his grasp on reality. In her opinion, some of the buildings would blow over in a good breeze. "As they aren't part of the protected Victorian district, the owners can do what they like with them."

"If you'll pardon the expression, Your Honor, certain aspects of the town's planning stink. There's been no public input into this development. The mayor's on the board of the development company and there's something very wrong with that picture. If we don't take a stand now, Spruce Lake could wind up full of concrete condos and shopping malls. Once those buildings are demolished, we won't be able to get them back. Our town's unique heritage should be preserved and I'm prepared to do anything to ensure that."

Despite his casual appearance, Becky conceded he was both articulate and public-spirited. "Your passion is admirable if a little misguided, sir. You vandalized private property and you'll have to be punished for it."

"Your Honor? If I could speak in my brother's favor."

Becky inclined her head.

The deputy scowled at his brother. "Will tends to be impetuous. Sometimes his enthusiasm gets in the way of his good intentions."

The court audience murmured their assent.

"In spite of how irresponsibly he acted last night, Will's a fine person... This was his first offence and, ah, he's extremely kind to animals, children and the elderly."

"Deputy O'Malley, that's *enough.*" Becky was losing her patience. She consulted the documents, then returned her attention to Will. "It states here that you entered private property and let the air out of the demolition vehicles' tires."

He grinned, as though enormously pleased with his achievement. "Yes, ma'am."

"Why?" she asked, and reached for a glass of water to cover the hoarseness in her voice. Surely he wasn't trying to flirt with her?

"The development company moved in their equipment, although the contract for sale hasn't closed yet. To prevent them from demolishing anything, a number of concerned citizens formed a human chain around the buildings while I flattened all the tires."

When the audience cheered, Becky surmised most of them were probably part of that "human chain."

She banged her gavel and ordered, "Silence!" Fixing him with her sternest glare, she said, "You also painted unflattering messages on their vehicles."

The audience laughed and several wolf-whistled. "Way to go, boy," Frank Farquar yelled, and Louella gave a snort of agreement.

Becky swore she could see steam rising from Matt O'Malley's ears. "What's that blasted pig still doing here?" she hissed at the bailiff.

"Louella is your next case. She ate the giant pumpkin Frank's cousin Hank was raising for the county fair."

Becky glanced at her list and groaned. She'd skimmed over the wretched pig's name when perusing her caseload and failed to notice that Louella—listed as Ms. L. Farquar—was appearing on another offence. She fought the urge to put her forehead on the bench and bang it. Instead, she made a note to her clerk that pigs were *not* to be listed as defendants in her court—only their owners! That done, she made another note to check if the county ordinances covered reasons for disposing of pesky pigs. Louella was Public Nuisance Number One. *That pig is going to end up bacon if she doesn't start behaving herself,* she decided. Louella had the exasperating habit of causing an enormous amount of damage wherever she waddled. Any normal person would leave his pig at home, rather than taking it shopping, but Frank Farquar treated Louella like an overindulged child.

She closed her eyes and uttered a silent oath. *If I can put up with this hick town for six months, I'll have a better chance of being posted to a court in Denver—or* anywhere *that isn't Spruce Lake. Provided I don't end up going crazy first!*

She'd rashly accepted her first judicial appointment after having worked in a Denver law firm for several years. When she'd failed to make partner for the third time—the job being given yet again to a male associate—Becky resigned and applied for the vacancy in Peaks County, viewing the six-month posting as a stepping-stone to a position in a metropolitan court. In the four weeks she'd been in Spruce Lake—standing in for Judge Emily Stevens while she took maternity leave—Becky had earned a reputation as a straight talker who meted out justice with a dose of blunt advice on how to stay out of her court in future. *Not that any of them seem to take it,* she thought, surveying the full courtroom. She couldn't wait to get back to the city—any city—where people weren't permitted to bring their pigs to court.

"May I say something, Your Honor?"

"Do you really think that's wise?"

Will O'Malley smiled again and Becky clenched her fists in an effort to get control of herself—and the court. Failure to do so meant this case could come back to haunt her forever. "What?" she snapped.

"I used a water-based paint, so it shouldn't be too difficult to clean up."

The man was incorrigible. How could he possibly be related to Matt O'Malley? "That's very gratifying to hear because *you're* going to scrub every one of those vehicles so clean, they'll look like they just came from the showroom."

The deputy coughed politely. "What?" she demanded.

"They did just come from the showroom, Judge."

Becky could feel a monumental headache brewing. Maybe she should adjourn court for the rest of the day. Better still, go on permanent sick leave—preferably until her term in Spruce Lake was up. She took off her glasses and frowned at the defendant. "Don't you have any respect for other people's property?"

He managed to look indignant. "Of course I do. It's the reason I didn't use spray paint. I was trying to make a point and get publicity for our cause."

"Vandalizing expensive equipment does not make for good publicity. There are more effective ways to get your point across without breaking the law. Since you feel so strongly, why not approach the company about buying back the buildings?"

"I've considered that, Judge, but I don't have the financial resources."

Obviously, he wouldn't. The guy might be dazzlingly good-looking, but he was a dreamer. Like so many troublemakers, Will O'Malley was full of high ideals and no real substance to back them up. Pity. Because there was something about this particular troublemaker that troubled her libido. After rubbing the bridge of her nose, she put her glasses back on and said,

"You're to clean up the equipment you've vandalized within the next forty-eight hours. I'm also assigning you community service. Do you have a job?"

He shifted his feet and, for the first time since entering her courtroom, his bravado seemed to desert him.

She removed her glasses again. "Mr. O'Malley?"

WILL WISHED SHE'D PUT her glasses back on. She was too darned pretty to be a judge and he was having difficulty concentrating.

His former career had been guaranteed to have women the world over flirting outrageously with him. He was sure that the judge, like any warm-blooded woman, would be impressed. But he didn't want to talk about it. Not since the avalanche.

"Ah, I'm between jobs at the moment, Your Honor," he said, ignoring Matt's groan of resignation.

"In that case, what *skills* do you have that might be of use to the community?" She put her glasses back on and picked up a pen as though ready to take copious notes on his potential *skills*.

Will had a college degree but no truly useful skills. Until today, that hadn't bothered him. Until today, he hadn't met a woman he wanted to impress as much as the new judge.

"What was your most recent job?" she prompted.

"Tell her!" Matt said under his breath.

There was nothing else for it; he'd have to come clean. "I was a ski-movie actor," he said, squirming with embarrassment. The movies were short on dialogue—long on action and death-defying stunts. Strange how he'd only come to realize that in the past couple of months.

The judge paused in her note-taking and glanced up at him.

"You're a *ski-movie* actor?" Her tone told him exactly what she thought of that.

"Yes, ma'am. Although it's more stunt work than acting," he said, trying to downplay the glamour image associated with acting. Stunt work sounded as though he had a genuine career. He named some box-office successes. "Perhaps you've heard of *Vertical Slide? Extreme Dreams? Aspen Altitude?*"

The judge blinked. *Guess not.* Although it was tremendously lucrative, he wouldn't be going back to the movies. He'd traveled for ten years doing what he loved most—skiing the world's extreme terrain—but an avalanche had nearly claimed his life during shooting in the Andes two months ago. He'd been caught in dozens of avalanches before and, tragically, had friends die in them, but this time he'd come too close to death. Trapped and slowly suffocating while he awaited rescue, he'd reflected on his life and how pointless his career really was. Sure, the viewers enjoyed the action and probably the scenery, too, but the lifestyle was shallow, based on thrill-seeking, looking cool and never putting down roots. What had he really achieved that was worthwhile? What had he given back to his community? What would his epitaph say?

"I've retired from that line of work," he murmured.

"So you have a lot of time on your hands?"

Will winced. He wasn't used to sitting still. "Yes, ma'am."

"Then what are you good at that could be utilized by the local community?" she asked, sounding exasperated.

"Skiing, meeting women and ironing."

Will ignored Matt's glare. It was true—he enjoyed ironing. He'd gotten up to more than his share of mischief as a kid and his mom's punishment of choice was to make him do the ironing for their family of seven. In the process, he'd become an expert. Even Matt was impressed by his skill with an iron. He'd offer Matt several hours of free ironing to make up for the embarrassment he'd caused him over the protest.

"Maybe I could work at the information kiosk on Main Street?" he suggested. "I know a lot about the town."

"IRONING?" BECKY SAID, deliberately ignoring his suggestion regarding the information kiosk. She suspected he thought working there would be an excellent way of meeting women. The notion of a defendant—particularly this one—spending his community service flirting annoyed her. What annoyed her even more was her ridiculous, bordering-on-jealous contemplation of him flirting with other women.

"Ahh…Judge? I don't think that's a good idea—"

"*Deputy O'Malley!*" she snapped. "Please do *not* interrupt me." Returning her attention to the defendant, she fixed him with a glare that brooked no argument. "In addition to cleaning the development company's vehicles, you'll complete fifty hours of community service.

"As you apparently enjoy the company of senior citizens *and* have no real qualifications, you can do the ironing and shovel snow at the Twilight Years Retirement Home. You have one month to complete your assigned service. Is that clear?"

"Yes, ma'am."

Becky wished he'd stop calling her that, especially in that lazy drawl of his. It woke long-buried desires. She'd been so busy with her career and raising her young son—the result of her short-lived marriage—that sex and romance simply weren't on her agenda. Yet from the moment Will O'Malley had looked up at her and smiled, she'd felt a bolt of sexual awareness she hadn't experienced in a very long time—if ever.

She checked his details. He was thirty-two—four years younger than she was. Definitely not what Becky wanted in her life—a younger man, especially one who was irresponsible and had no respect for authority or the law. A charming rogue was *not* the answer to her sexual frustration. Not that she was aware she had any until he'd walked into her courtroom. She needed to get him out of there, fast. "If there's nothing further—"

"Well, I do have a question…"

"Yes, Mr. O'Malley?"

"Would you have dinner with me tonight?"

Becky blinked. Surely she hadn't heard him correctly. "Excuse me?" she said, and tried to ignore the warm flush climbing up her chest.

"I asked if you'd go out with me tonight."

The court audience leaned forward, eagerly anticipating her response.

Will O'Malley was without doubt the best-looking defendant who'd ever stood before her. The fact that he'd pleaded guilty straight up—rather than offer a host of excuses—impressed her. But he *was* a defendant and strictly off-limits.

Furious that her body was telling her one thing, while her brain told her another, Becky answered him more harshly than she'd intended. "No, Mr. O'Malley, I won't," she said and slammed down her gavel. "Get out of my court!"

Chapter Two

"That went better than I expected," Will said as he and Matt walked outside into the crisp winter morning.

Snow had fallen overnight, turning the town into a perfect Christmas card scene. Skiers trudged along the sidewalks, headed for the slopes, while sightseers gazed into shop fronts, admiring the Christmas displays. Carols sounded merrily from the tourist office. The holidays were only a couple of weeks away—Will's favorite time of year.

Matt sighed. "Define *better than you expected.* You've been assigned fifty hours of community service and had the judge very publicly turn you down for a date. Doesn't anything ever get you down?"

Will shrugged. "Nothing I can think of at the moment—apart from losing those old buildings." He couldn't tell Matt about the avalanche and the nightmares. Not yet.

"Don't you feel humiliated?"

"Nope. I deserved the punishment and I'll enjoy spending time at the old folks' home. Lots of interesting characters there. As for the delectable judge, she'll come around."

Matt rubbed his chin. "I'm not so sure. She keeps to herself." He paused. "And don't you dare even *think* of pursuing her and then take off on another one of your crazy adventures, leaving the rest of us to pick up the pieces."

Will opened his mouth to answer the accusations but, as usual,

Matt hadn't finished telling him off. "And what the hell was all that, 'I'm going to marry that woman someday,' nonsense?"

Will grinned and said, *"Bashert."*

Matt's eyes narrowed. His voice dripping with mock sarcasm, he said, "You spent two weeks skiing in Israel last winter and now you speak fluent Hebrew?"

"Actually, it's Yiddish. And I'm far from fluent. *Bashert* is the instant recognition of one's soul mate."

"I'm aware of what it is! It happened for me with Sally," Matt said testily, referring to the deep and instant love he'd felt for his wife. But a drunk driver had killed Sally two years earlier. She was seven months pregnant at the time.

"And Dad with Mom," Will said, trying to distract Matt from grieving over Sally. He wasn't comfortable with deep emotion. "Seems like *bashert*'s an O'Malley tradition."

"Not where Luke's concerned."

Their oldest brother's ex-wife, Tory, had made Luke's life a living hell. Although he'd been divorced for a couple of years now, Luke was still a grouch.

"True. But I'm positive about the judge."

Matt raised a sardonic eyebrow. "Really? You haven't checked out her other assets. For all you know, hidden behind that bench might be three hairy legs and a pointed tail."

Will grinned at his brother's rare attempt at levity. "You've been reading too many of those kiddie fantasy novels to young Sash." Sasha was one of their much-adored nieces and Luke's oldest daughter.

"Speaking of children, the judge has one of her own."

"She's married?" Will felt sick to his stomach.

Matt placed a hand on his shoulder. "Relax. She's divorced. But I'm sure the thought of having to compete with another *child—*" Matt emphasized the word "—for the judge's attention, should be enough to quench your fires."

Ignoring the jibe, he said, "A kid? How d'you know?"

"Because I listen to people."

"So you've had the opportunity to chat with the object of my affections?"

"I have."

"And?"

"And what?"

"Is she as immune to your charms as she's trying to be to mine?"

"I think you could confidently say she's completely immune to your charms."

"On the contrary. I think she's intrigued."

"Yeah. Right. Face it, buddy, Judge McBride is way too disciplined for someone as unruly as you. Still, stranger things have happened—especially in Spruce Lake." He glanced at his watch. "I have to go back to work, but before I do, I've got to ask—this protest movement you're getting together...who's heading it up?"

Will puffed out his chest. "Me, of course. And we've called it Save Our Buildings or SOB, 'cause it'd be a crying shame to lose them."

Matt shook his head. "Trust you to come up with such an absurd acronym. Can I be blunt with you?"

"Fire away."

"There seems to be a groundswell of support for your crazy idea—"

Will threw up his hands. "It is *not* crazy!"

"Okay...let's call it well-meaning but totally irrational."

Will nodded. "That's much better." He enjoyed sparring with Matt.

"What I'm trying to get across to you is that this protest—if you can get enough support for it—has the potential of becoming huge, and if you walk away without following through, you're going to disappoint a lot of people. No, more than that, you're going to hurt them because they believe in you."

"I told you I'm here to stay. Why do you doubt me?"

"Because I know your past record! And when it finally gets through your thick skull that the judge isn't interested, you'll head off to the ends of the earth on another harebrained adventure."

Will was about to repeat that he was here to stay, but Matt was on a roll.

"You breeze into town, stopping for a few days, before you fly off to make yet another movie in some far-off location," Matt ranted. "You've never shown any interest in sticking with anything worthwhile. Why change now?"

Although his tirade stung, Matt was right. Not so long ago, Will wouldn't have been ready to hear it, or to agree with Matt. But his brush with death had changed Will's view of the world and his place in it. The avalanche had made him realize the carefree days of his extended youth were over. Did he really want to spend his life flying around the world, engaging in increasingly more daring stunts, living out of a suitcase? The answer was a resounding *no.*

He'd come home—to the certain safety of Spruce Lake—determined to settle in his hometown. Unfortunately, he hadn't figured out how he'd make a living here. The judge had underlined something he already knew: Apart from being able to ski near-vertical cliffs, he didn't have any real skills. And therefore no alternative career prospects.

However, discovering that the old buildings were threatened with demolition had confirmed Spruce Lake was an intrinsic part of him and saving them was a cause worth fighting for. "I won't have our town's heritage destroyed by a bunch of shiny Tonka toys!" he declared.

"That's what you say now. Next week might be a different story."

Will gritted his teeth. "I said *I'm here to stay.*"

"Fine." Matt's curled lip told Will he doubted his convictions. "If you're as determined as you claim to be, I'll do whatever I can. And if you're so hell-bent on dating the judge, then let me talk to her on your behalf. I'll tell her you're a generally well-behaved citizen who's temporarily taken leave of his senses. She'd believe it coming from me. She *might* even let you date her, then."

She probably would, but that'd be cheating. His big brother

couldn't help sticking up for him. Protecting him—protecting *anyone*—came naturally to Matt.

"Thanks for the offer, but I want to win her over myself. She's already intrigued. Soon, she won't be able to resist me, you'll see."

"And you figured this out in your brief yet humiliating encounter this morning?" Matt shook his head. "Your overconfidence astounds me, Will. And the protest, what about that? And your job? The one you pretended you don't have? What was that about, saying you're 'between jobs'? And speaking of your job, you've been here nearly two weeks. It's winter in case you hadn't noticed. Prime ski-movie shooting season."

Will disregarded Matt's sarcasm. "Like I said in court, I quit the movies." He held up his hands to allay Matt's questions as to why. "SOB will keep me busy." When he saw Matt about to argue, he said, "I'm not going to suddenly take off, okay?"

Matt leaned against his vehicle. "Do you have a plan—apart from continuing to vandalize the development company's property?"

"I do."

"And?"

Pleased by Matt's interest, he said, "I'm holding a fundraising barbecue."

Matt's raised eyebrows told Will what he thought of that. "And plan B would be?"

"There *is* no plan B! What's wrong with plan A?"

Matt indicated the snow-covered street. "It's winter. No one has barbecues in the middle of winter."

"All the more reason to have one. People hankering for barbecue will come from all over."

"And where do you plan to hold this event? Close off Main Street like they do during the summer barbecue festival? You'll need a permit and we both know how much you hate dealing with bureaucracy."

"Don't need one if we hold it at the ranch."

Matt rolled his eyes. "Yeah, right. Running it by Luke will

be harder than getting a permit from the town. Good luck with that." He pushed away from his vehicle. "Do you want a ride somewhere?"

"Thanks, but I need to stretch my legs and get some fresh air. Then I'll walk over to the Twilight Years and start my community service."

Matt clapped him on the shoulder. "Good idea. I can't fault your work ethic, buddy, but I wish you were a bit more conventional."

Will raised his hands in jest. "Then I'd be like you."

Matt let the mild insult go as he shook Will's hand, then climbed into his vehicle and lowered the window. "I just had a thought."

"You, Matt O'Malley, had a spontaneous moment?"

Matt started his car. "Okay, if you're going to be insulting, I'll go."

Will reached in and switched off the ignition. "Sorry, couldn't stop myself." He leaned on the door frame and said, "Shoot."

"You know that ranch land you bought ten years back?"

"Yup."

"I think you'll find it's appreciated considerably in value."

Will was lost. "Meaning?"

"Meaning that if you're serious about saving those buildings, then get the land valued. You might be able to sell it and raise enough to buy the buildings from the development company yourself."

"You're joking."

"Have you ever known me to joke?"

Good point. "But this is crazy. I paid peanuts for it."

"Times have changed. You might be surprised by what it's worth."

"Nice idea. But I'm keeping the land as a wildlife corridor. Where would the elk graze and the bears collect berries to get them through the winter and the lynx hunt if I sold it? I couldn't have some rancher fencing it off, grazing cows and horses and shooting anything that eats the grass—or the livestock."

"You know as well as I do it's too small to be a viable ranch, but in the past couple of years they've started developing ranchettes for people who want to be near a town but also want the luxury of extra land. That valley is the prettiest around and people would pay a premium to live there."

Ranchettes? Will shuddered. "Even if I could raise the money to buy the buildings—provided the development company would consider selling them—I'd have the problem of a bunch of disgruntled elk and bears." He ignored Matt's sardonic look and explained, "I couldn't live with myself if I sold it to someone to carve up into tiny plots. Sorry, Matt, but it doesn't work for me."

"Five- to ten-acre lots aren't tiny. You're never going to graze that land. You're allergic to horses, remember?"

At the reminder of his allergy, Will sneezed, then scratched his shoulder. "Speaking of allergies, can I stay with you for a while?" Will suspected Luke had put him in the apartment above the stables on purpose, hoping he'd move on—preferably to another country. The smell of hay and horses had him sneezing for at least an hour every morning, and Luke kept hinting that if Will wasn't doing any useful work around the ranch, he should leave.

"I'd rather have my teeth pulled without benefit of anesthetic than share living quarters with you *ever* again," Matt said.

"There's no need to get personal. I've grown up since the last time we lived together."

"Not enough to let you move in," he muttered.

True, he'd pulled a few shots in his past, and Matt had a *very* long memory. Unfortunately, there was a shortage of rental accommodation in town—especially with the holidays just around the corner. His land had a burned-out farmhouse that wasn't habitable. Pitching a tent and living in it during winter wasn't feasible. Come spring, he intended to start work on a cabin, but until then he was pretty much homeless. And car-less. He'd have to do something about that, too. Building the cabin would prove to his family *and* the town that Will O'Malley had grown up and was going to stick around and become a contributing member of the community. "Selling my land isn't an option."

Matt shrugged. "Suit yourself." He started up the car. "Take care, Will. If you need anything, you know where to find me. In the meantime, keep out of trouble, okay?"

After waving Matt off, Will headed down the street, his mind filled with plans: saving the buildings, getting Matt elected sheriff, designing a log cabin, locating happy homes for old Miss P.'s dogs, finding a job that didn't involve going anywhere near the mountain—or horses, buying a car, completing his community service without burning down the old folks' home, talking Luke into holding the fundraiser at the ranch, and most importantly, getting the judge to have dinner with him.

Chapter Three

Two days later, and no closer to a solution regarding either his career future or how he could save the buildings, Will was strolling along Main Street, admiring the Christmas displays, when a car pulled up beside him. Louella's piggy snout hung out the window, sniffing the chilled air.

Frank Farquar plucked an enormous cigar from his mouth and asked, "Off to help out at the old folks' home again?"

Frank's Aztec Red 1959 Cadillac Series 62 complete with tail fins of extraordinary proportions was a legend of a car. From the front of its shiny chrome double grille to the rear rocket-inspired, double bullet-head taillights, the Caddy was Frank's pride and joy. Frank owned the rock quarry ten miles past the south end of town but, miraculously, not a speck of dust ever marred the Caddy's paintwork. Will hadn't yet got around to buying himself a vehicle. A car like Frank's was one to be proud of—impractical but impressive.

He ducked to look in the front window and got a wet kiss from Louella. "Yup. Going that way, Mr. F.?"

"For you, boy, I'd drive all the way to Denver. Hop in."

Respecting Louella's pride of place up front, Will got into the backseat. "Nice outfit, Lou," he remarked, referring to her snappy tartan vest and scarf, and got a snort of appreciation in return. He figured Frank's dressing up Louella had something to do with the fact that he was a bachelor who'd never had the chance to raise kids of his own. Given how eccentric Frank was, Will wasn't surprised he'd never married, in spite of his reported wealth.

"I see you cleaned up them demolition vehicles," Frank said around the cigar he chewed but never lit.

"With a lot of help from the local Boy Scout troop." Will was grateful to them. Cleaning off the water-based paint in the subfreezing temperature hadn't been easy. The kids were selling Christmas trees in their lot across the street and came over to offer their services in exchange for his autograph and some photos with him.

"Has the judge come to her senses about dating you, boy?"

"Not yet, Mr. F., but I'm optimistic."

"That you are. Never met anyone more optimistic than you. Even Lou—" he slapped his pig's back with affection "—can get a bit down in the mouth at times, but I don't think I ever seen you not smilin'."

Will would be celebrating his thirty-second birthday next month, yet people still saw him as a boy. It had never bothered him before, but now it didn't sit so well. His old school buddies were all married; most had kids. That guaranteed weekends spent mowing lawns and taking kids to Little League, neighborhood barbecues and friendly softball matches stretching into the summer evenings. And nights curled up beside a woman who loved you. In truth, most of his old friends had found a contentment that had always eluded Will.

He and Frank were a lot alike—lonely bachelors—although Will hadn't yet resorted to driving around with a farm animal in his front seat for company. The town's population numbered over two thousand, but the pool of eligible men the judge might date—*if* she ever dated—was small. Provided his brother Adam didn't move back anytime soon. The career-oriented judge was sure to be impressed by a dedicated, overmuscled firefighter.

Will put that unwelcome thought out of his mind and concentrated on Frank. He and Mrs. Carmichael, the florist, had been high school sweethearts. She'd gone off to college in

Denver and eventually married and settled there. Widowed many years later, she'd come home to Spruce Lake and opened a florist shop. But the former sweethearts had barely spoken to each other since her return.

"Here we are, boy." Frank jolted Will from his musings as they pulled up outside the Twilight Years.

Frank turned in his seat and held out a wad of money.

"What's this for?"

"The Save Our Buildings fund," Frank said. "I had this in my mattress. I was figurin' maybe we could raise money for the town to buy back the old buildings. Like the judge suggested."

Will was touched. "Thanks, Mr. F., but I doubt there's enough money in the whole town to do that." His hastily devised plan during the protest was simply to raise funds to fight the development company in court and convince them to rethink their demolition of the buildings.

"You'd be surprised how much money there is in this town," Frank was saying. "Folks just don't have nothin' worthwhile to spend it on." He proffered the wad of cash again.

Will held up his hands. "Ah, I appreciate the offer, but I don't feel comfortable walking around with all that money. Let's open an account down at the bank, okay?"

Frank considered his words, then nodded. "Good idea."

A thought occurred to Will. "Mrs. C. has a donation tin on her shop counter, but this is way too much to leave in there. As SOB treasurer, I know she'd be over the moon with a donation like this. You should be a cosignatory on the account with her."

"I doubt Edna would want to sign anything with me. We don't exactly get along. In fact, you could say she hates me."

Poor Frank, he had it bad, Will surmised, observing his trembling lip. "I'm sure if you worked together on the campaign, she'd see a side of you that will please her beyond measure."

"You think?"

Will climbed out of the Caddy. "I'm sure she'll appreciate your generous donation to our cause," he said, giving Louella's head a scratch.

He was positive that Mrs. C. would appreciate the donation. He wasn't so certain she'd forgive Frank for whatever wrong he'd committed forty years earlier.

LATER THAT AFTERNOON, Will was walking old Miss Patterson's five dogs, who were a real handful. Planning moves on the development company, how to sweet-talk Luke into holding a barbecue at the ranch and walking a pack of dogs didn't mix.

Miss Patterson had never married, nor had children of her own, but she was well-loved around town. The dogs were her life and Will always enjoyed visiting with the cheerful octogenarian and her "boys" whenever he was home. She not only made the world's best chocolate chip cookies and was an accomplished watercolor artist, but possessed a vast knowledge of the Spruce Lake area and its history.

During the protest, as she'd bravely faced the demolition vehicles charging toward her, she'd asked Will if he could help her find good homes for the dogs. At the time, he feared it was because Miss Patterson thought she was going to be run down and killed. But she'd explained that the dogs were getting to be too much for her and wanted them adopted into loving homes.

"Whoa there, boys," he warned as the dogs dragged him along Main Street. Dermott the Irish setter, Dugald the Scottish terrier and Henri the toy poodle were attached by their leashes to his left hand. Edward, the Old English sheepdog and Charles the bull terrier's leashes were clasped firmly in his right. No wonder Miss P. needed a hip replacement, Will mused. The dogs were nearly tearing his arms out of their sockets and his feet were planted so firmly in the snow he was practically skiing behind them.

The toot of a car's horn had all of them pricking up their ears. When they spotted Louella sailing past with her snout stuck out the window of Frank Farquar's Caddy, they took off after her. Five dogs and a man became a blur in the shop windows as they shot along Main Street in pursuit of Louella, squealing her approval out the window.

"Shut up, Louella, you idiot pig!" Will yelled as he yanked

on the leashes with all his might, while pedestrians scattered like snowflakes before them. His command had little or no effect on Charles who continued racing down the street, dragging Edward and Will.

Frank turned at the corner of Main and Jefferson, the Caddy fishtailing on the slippery street. Now the car was out of sight, Dermott forgot about Louella and slowed to a trot, while Dugald spotted a fire hydrant to relieve himself on. Henri, exhausted from the effort of keeping up with the much larger dogs, dropped to his stomach. Edward flopped down, too. His considerable weight had the effect of bringing everyone else to a standstill, although the forward motion of Will's body took a moment to catch up.

Trying to avoid treading on tiny Henri, Will leaped into the air, twisted sideways, collected a potted Christmas tree complete with decorations, then fell backward over Edward. His head hit the snow-covered sidewalk with such force he saw stars. He lay on his back staring up at the sky through the Christmas tree branches, with Edward breathing Old English sheepdoggie breath on his face.

JUDGE BECKY MCBRIDE witnessed all this from the courthouse steps.

After a long day, exacerbated by Louella getting up to further mischief, she'd escaped the courtroom madhouse only to find more animals misbehaving outside.

Will O'Malley saw her and scrambled to his feet. "Afternoon, Your Honor," he said and attempted to unwind himself from the mass of dogs, their leads and, she noted curiously, a bedraggled Christmas tree laced with silver tinsel. Finally free of the leashes, he gave a couple of commands to the dogs and they walked with their heads held high toward her.

Fond of Scotties, she bent to pat the Scottish terrier. They seemed to have hardy, courageous temperaments. The other dogs nuzzled her hand eagerly. Becky laughed, delighted by their antics.

"Hello! Aren't you gorgeous?" she told the dogs and

scratched behind their ears, but the Scottie was the most insistent about getting her attention.

"That's Dugald," Will O'Malley told her. "He's very bossy and a good watchdog. This is Edward—" he indicated the Old English sheepdog "—he's a lazy lump and eats too much, but he makes a nice footrest in front of the fire on cold nights. Dermott's the setter. He's got no brains whatsoever, but he loves children. Charles needs psychotherapy—" he pointed to the bull terrier "—because he's in love with Louella Farquar. And Henri's convinced he's related to Louis XVI and doesn't much care for walks."

"He's wearing fur-lined booties *and* a fur doggie coat," she said. "The question is *why?*"

"Seriously, he thinks he's related to royalty—hence, the fur coat. *Fake* fur," he pointed out. "And the booties are to protect his dear little feet from the cold."

Becky was charmed by his genuine affection for the animals. "Why are you walking so many dogs? Have you started a dog-walking business since we last met?" She bent to pet the dogs again.

"Nope. Although your suggestion has merit. Would you date me if I had a dog-walking business?" he asked.

Becky stood, ready to make her departure. "No."

"I'm going to keep asking, you know that, don't you?"

"And I'm going to keep saying no, regardless of what sort of business you have, Mr. O'Malley. Good day." She turned to leave.

"They belong to Miss Patterson up on Lincoln Street," he said, stalling her. "She's getting too frail to handle them all herself."

Becky turned back, realizing she hadn't discovered why he was walking so many dogs.

"She could probably cope with Henri. But she'll have to give the others away and it's going to break her heart. These dogs are her children. Imagine how that would tear you up, having to give away a child of yours, let alone four of them."

Becky didn't want to consider how desolate she'd feel about losing Nicolas. In truth, she was relieved Graham had rejected their son when they'd received his diagnosis. It meant he'd never show up on her doorstep demanding custody or even visitation rights.

"We had a long talk about the boys' futures and Miss P.'s asked me to inquire around for good homes. Would you be interested in adopting Dugald, by any chance?"

She bent to pet the Scottie again. Nicolas begged her for a puppy on a weekly basis. He'd hinted it would be the perfect Christmas present. Becky didn't have room in her life for a dog, so that particular Christmas wish would remain unfulfilled.

She shook her head, but she was touched by Will O'Malley's caring attitude. His brother had testified he was kind to old people and animals, and it was obviously the truth. She'd sensed in court that there was more to the man than his misconduct would indicate. And to his credit, she'd seen him scrubbing the demolition vehicles the very evening she'd handed down her punishment. A group of Boy Scouts were helping him and seemed to be enjoying themselves and his company. Thankfully, he'd been so engrossed in his task, he hadn't noticed her passing by. Earlier, she'd seen him standing outside the supermarket entrance, dressed as Santa and ringing a bell, collecting money for a local charity. She couldn't fault his community spirit.

She glanced up from the dogs to find him appraising her openly. "What are you looking at?"

"You. You're gorgeous."

Becky felt herself blush to the roots of her hair. No man had ever paid her such a bold compliment. "No, I'm not."

"Oh, yes, you are," he insisted. "Come out with me tonight?"

There was no way she was going anywhere with Will O'Malley, no matter how good-looking or how kind to animals and the elderly he was. And no matter how many roses he sent her.

Becky had been delighted by the first delivery. Then she'd read the card and discovered who'd sent them.

The certain knowledge that encouraging him would be disastrous for her career advancement made it easy to reject his overtures. Will O'Malley was Trouble.

She was about to turn down his invitation, when the dogs started to walk around them—in opposite directions. They strained against their leashes, forcing Becky against Will O'Malley's body and tightening his arms around her.

"Oh!" she cried as their bodies touched intimately from chest to knee, courtesy of the dogs.

"This is nice," he murmured and bent to kiss her. Startled, Becky turned her head to the side to avoid letting their mouths make contact. Then wished she hadn't. The feel of his warm lips brushing her cheek had her wanting more. But this was madness. She leaned away from him as best she could. "Mr. O'Malley! Get your hands off me."

"We're not in court anymore, darlin'," he drawled in a tone that was guaranteed to make any woman weak in the knees—her included. "So why don't you call me Will?"

She pushed against his chest. "How about if I don't? Now, *get your hands off me,*" she repeated in a low growl.

He looked pointedly at where her hands lay against his chest. "Seems like you're the one who's got her hands all over me. Mine are only around you because of the dogs."

She glanced down to see that her fingers had curled into his shirtfront as though seeking greater contact.

"Oh!" She pulled them back abruptly.

"Don't be frightened. I was enjoying myself, and judging by the flush on your pretty cheeks and that tiny pulse throbbing in your neck—" he grinned with mischievous intent and gazed into her eyes "—I do believe you were enjoying yourself, too."

She was lost in the depths of his eyes. Chocolate-brown eyes... He was too smooth for words. Too dangerous, too damned attractive. She needed to take control. *Control* was what she thrived on. It gave meaning to her life—helped her cope in any situation.

Forcing strength back into her legs, she stood up to her full height. "Why...you arrogant...*pest!* How *dare* you assume such a thing. Now, get the dogs unraveled and let me go. I have a reputation to uphold. I can't be seen being manhandled in the street by a…a delinquent."

"So quit your job and come live with me. Then I can manhandle you all you want," he said, as if her concerns about her reputation didn't matter one iota to him.

Her cheeks burned with anger.

"Because that's what you really want, isn't it, darlin'? You *want* me to hold you…and touch you…and kiss every inch of your beautiful body…."

She swallowed, her mouth suddenly dry. A moment ago, she'd wanted to throttle him. But in all honesty, what he was suggesting was *exactly* what she wanted him to do. Hadn't she dreamed of it every night since she'd met him?

She gave herself a mental shake. What was she *thinking?* Letting him *touch* her, *kiss* her… A flutter of anticipation filled her at the notion of being seduced by Will O'Malley. He'd probably prove a very thorough—and satisfying—lover.

But he wasn't for her. Absolutely not! As an official of the law, she had to maintain her reputation. It was part of the reason she'd become a judge. Judges were highly respected members of society, and she wanted respect more than anything in her life.

The humiliation of attending court with her father, holding him up because he was so drunk, was deeply imprinted in her psyche. Becky had been fifteen, vulnerable, angry and confused. But when she'd seen the judge sitting behind his bench and being called "Your Honor" by everyone present, Becky knew the career she wanted to pursue—a career that *commanded* respect. She'd hated being the outcast at school, the new girl wearing thrift-shop clothes because the family moved from town to town and was too destitute, because of her father's gambling and drinking, to afford anything new. Tears sprang to her eyes at the memory.

HER TEARS SHOCKED WILL. Surely she didn't feel threatened by his playful advances? He gave the dogs a sharp command and they unwound themselves and their prisoners. The judge took a step back and glanced at the crowd gathering on the sidewalk, and then at him. Her face was almost redder than her hair.

"I'm sorry," he whispered. "I didn't mean to scare you."

Her chin came up. "You didn't scare me, Mr. O'Malley. I'm not frightened of anything. Least of all *you.*" She turned on her heel and stalked off down the sidewalk.

He gazed at her retreating back. She might have claimed nothing scared her, but Will was damned sure she was afraid of *something.*

ALTHOUGH SHE'D MARCHED off after their humiliating encounter, Becky's legs weren't as steady as she would've liked. The trip down unhappy-memory lane had rattled her, and she'd let down her guard. "Damn!" she said and swiped at her cheeks, hoping no one would notice the tears that refused to stop welling in her eyes.

She turned down her street, head low as she avoided other pedestrians. She'd felt like a complete spectacle there in the middle of Main Street being held by Will O'Malley for the entire world to see!

Nicolas wasn't home—he was still at the hydrotherapy pool doing a session with his physical therapist. For once, she was home alone and could indulge in a bit of self-pity.

After lighting the fire, she poured a glass of pinot noir and curled up in a corner of the sofa, tucking her legs underneath her. The room was pleasantly furnished. She'd brought a few decorative pieces with her, but the quaint Victorian house was fully furnished. That meant Becky was able to rent out her renovated loft apartment in Denver for the six months they'd be in Spruce Lake. She'd bought it with part of her divorce settlement. The rest she'd invested in Nicolas's college fund, although she'd have to dip into that to pay for the exclusive school for gifted children he'd be entering next fall when they returned to Denver.

The wine's warmth seeped through her, calming her nerves.

The sooner she got out of this town, where everyone knew everyone else—and their business!—the better. Whatever had possessed her to accept the job here?

The spectators today had brought back unwanted memories from her past. The only memories Becky cherished from that long-ago time were of spending every spare moment at Ben Solomon's office learning about the law. The kindly lawyer had taken her under his wing and helped her apply for a scholarship to attend college and then law school on the East Coast—far away from her family. Sadly, Ben hadn't lived to see her graduate.

Her first job was with a prestigious Atlanta law firm where she'd met Graham Marcus, one of the firm's high-flying partners. Urbane and charming, he had a wide circle of friends. They'd worked on several cases together, dated occasionally and a few months later he'd asked her to marry him.

Flattered and desperate to have a family of her own, she'd agreed without seriously examining whether she loved him—or if, indeed, he really loved her. *Marry in haste, repent at leisure.* The proverb's words had come back to haunt her.

Three months after their wedding, Becky was pregnant. Dreaming that at last she'd have the family life she craved—she failed to notice something amiss in their marriage. When she discovered Graham had a mistress, the betrayal was so devastating she'd nearly miscarried. Graham begged her forgiveness. He put their unborn son's name on the waiting list for the same exclusive schools he'd attended and became the doting expectant father. But soon after Nicolas's birth, it was apparent that all was not quite right with the baby. When they received the diagnosis that Nicolas suffered from cerebral palsy and might never walk, Graham's interest in their son evaporated and he demanded Becky put him into permanent care.

Bewildered that he could instantly turn from loving their son to despising him, she'd packed her bags and left with Nicolas, determined her dear little boy would know only unconditional love and support.

She'd filed for divorce and custody of Nicolas—Graham

contested neither—and she'd had no contact with her ex-husband since.

Another man had let her down. She swore that would never happen again. She'd been a fool to forgive Graham his affair. She would never forgive him for rejecting their son.

And she had no intention of opening her heart to pain ever again.

Becky sipped her wine, allowing its warm glow to spread through her. But the warmth reminded her of Will O'Malley and how good his arms had felt around her. How *safe* she'd felt in his embrace. *I need to get out of this town, because he makes me yearn for things I can't have.*

She sipped more of the wine and thought, *Now, there's a man who'd head for the hills if he knew I had a physically challenged child.*

Chapter Four

"Have you heard anything from your ladylove yet, dear?" Mrs. Carmichael asked as Will cleaned up after repainting her shop.

He dried the paintbrushes and stored them. "Nope," he said. "But she'll come around."

He'd been doing odd jobs at the florist's for the past few days in between fulfilling his community service obligations at the Twilight Years Home. In payment, Mrs. C. sent him off to the courthouse with a dozen red roses every day. But instead of being shown into the judge's chambers, he'd had to leave them with the receptionist at the front desk. So far, he hadn't received any acknowledgment of either the flowers or the notes requesting a date that he'd hidden among the blooms.

"Maybe the judge doesn't like roses?" she suggested. "I could do some lovely spring bouquets."

Will picked up a cloth and wiped down the counter in front of him. "You're sweet, Mrs. C. One of Spruce Lake's living treasures."

She flapped a hand at him good-naturedly. "Get on with you, Will O'Malley. Like your dear papa, you've inherited the Irish blarney."

"Nope, it's true. Cross my heart." He did so, then bent to kiss her goodbye. "Toodle loo, Mrs. C. I'm off to see the mayor and walk Miss P.'s boys. And don't forget to call me if you need anything. Otherwise, I'll have to put you into the Twilight Years." He shook his finger at her.

"You're so insolent," she said with a laugh. "I always thought your mama was way too lenient with you. Good luck with the mayor. And don't forget, you're welcome to move into my upstairs apartment anytime, dear."

"Thanks, Mrs. C. I'm so done with Luke whining I'm underfoot at the ranch." He'd told her about the details of his latest conflicts with his oldest brother.

She shook her head, her voice full of compassion. "Ah, Luke. Like you, he has a heart of gold. Being the oldest of you boys, he takes on a lot of responsibility."

Luke was on the wrong side of thirty-five. Hardly a boy.

"He needs a wife to help him with the ranch and those dear little girls of his."

Considering Luke's unhappy marital history, Will didn't have much faith in his brother's taste in wives. He'd been cranky since the day he said, "I do." Since it was a shotgun wedding, Will could understand Luke's foul mood. Tory had set a trap for Luke that he couldn't see through at the time. However, the doomed marriage did produce three sweet little girls.

The shop's doorbell rang and in stepped Frank Farquar with Louella at his heels, sporting a pink tutu. Mrs. C. sucked in her breath.

"Edna." Frank removed his best black ten-gallon hat. It was Frank's *prosperous rancher* look. To Will's knowledge, the only time Frank had been anywhere near a cow was when he was barbecuing beef.

Will scratched Louella behind the ear, then busied himself with restacking some shelves out of Mrs. C.'s reach, figuring he should stay for a bit longer. After all, Frank might need his moral support.

"What can I do for you, *Mr.* Farquar?" she asked.

"I'd like a bunch of your most expensive flowers for someone very special."

Will was taken aback. Frank Farquar had a ladylove? Judging by the look on Mrs. C.'s face, that particular bit of gossip hadn't made its way down to her part of Main Street. Yet.

Yesterday, as he'd put up new shelves for her, Mrs. C. had related their story. She'd had such hopes for her and Frank all those years ago, yet he'd been too busy making a success of his rock quarry to get around to proposing marriage. She'd wondered how different her life would have been. Would they have had the children she'd so desperately wanted and been unable to have with her husband, Jeb Carmichael?

She expelled a sigh as though she'd been thinking the same thing as Will.

"You work too hard, Edna."

She bristled. "I do *not*. And I'll thank you to mind your own business." She plucked a bunch of pink-and-white Oriental lilies, ripe with perfume, from a bucket of water. "These are my most expensive blooms."

Lilies were Mrs. C.'s favorite and she always kept them in her store, saying their exotic scent cheered her, even on the bleakest days. It surprised Will that she'd recommended them for another woman.

Frank shrugged. "I dunno. Do you like 'em, Edna?"

"What's it matter what I think?" she snapped, then seemed to rein in her temper. "Of course I do. They're beautiful flowers. However, if you'd prefer roses, I can order some for you. Will has cleaned me out of roses this week."

Frank turned to Will. "I wondered where all those flowers at the courthouse came from. They from you, boy?"

"They sure are. Not that it's doing me much good. Yet."

"You're positive she'll like 'em?" Frank looked at Mrs. C. again.

"Of course she will! I'm a florist, and I know my business!"

Will detected an undercurrent of jealousy in her tone. This could be promising—if only Frank hadn't turned his attention to another woman.

"I'll take 'em."

"I haven't told you how much they are."

"I don't care. She's worth it."

Frank winked at Will. Mrs. C. saw it and fumed. In fact, Will noted, she was so mad, she doubled the price.

"That'll be eighty dollars. Would you like a card to go with them?"

Frank slapped two fifties on the counter, saying, "Keep the change, and yes, I'll take a card."

He chose a pen and started writing in the card. Mrs. C. tapped her foot. Will grinned at her. She glared back at him. A strategic retreat right about now would be a good idea, but Will couldn't drag himself away. Instead, he climbed the stepladder and pretended to wipe down a top shelf.

"There." Frank placed the card in the bouquet and stood back as if to admire his handiwork.

"If there's nothing else I can help you with, then you'll be going," Mrs. C. said in dismissal.

"Not so fast," Frank said, handing over the flowers.

"What are you doing?" she demanded.

"Read the card."

Scowling, she opened it and read aloud. "'Dearest Edna, Roses are red, violets are blue. My heart is so lonely, lonely for you.'"

Will's heart soared. But Mrs. C. looked as though she didn't know whether to laugh or be sick.

The sight of Louella munching on one of the buckets of brilliantly colored gerberas brought her back to the present. "Oh, you *naughty* pig!" she cried, picking up a broom to chase Louella off. Louella spotted her and squealed, charging toward the protection of Frank's legs. Unfortunately, she knocked over several flower-filled buckets and crashed into Will's ladder in her haste to escape.

The doorbell rang, announcing another customer, as Will tumbled off the ladder and landed on top of Louella who squealed even louder and rushed out the back of the shop. She headed into Mrs. Carmichael's living quarters, leaving a trail of wet trotter prints in her wake and Will lying half-dazed in a flower-strewn pool of water.

"You and your blasted *pig,* Frank Farquar! You should both

be locked up," Mrs. C. declared as Will felt himself all over for injuries. "Now look what she's done. *Get her out of my home!*"

"I can't understand this. I told her to be on her best behavior. Maybe she's jealous?" Frank muttered and went in pursuit of Louella.

The *jealous* comment only served to make Edna Carmichael madder. She picked up a vase and threw it at him. It hit the wall and smashed.

Will dragged his attention from the commotion at the back of the shop to the customer who'd entered through the front door.

The judge was standing there, her expression contemptuous as she stared at the scene of devastation.

Will scrambled to his feet. "I'm afraid you've caught me at a bad time."

"I wasn't coming to see you, Mr. O'Malley, but since you're here, I can deliver my message in person."

"I'm all ears." He offered one of his deep-dimpled grins, knowing from experience that women would forgive him anything if he smiled at them. Except maybe this particular woman...

The judge was unmoved by his overture. "Thank you for the flowers. Please don't send me any more," she said, then turned on her heel and left the store.

Will was puzzled. Why wouldn't a woman want flowers? His dad had wooed his mom with flowers. His mom had apparently been as difficult to date as the judge, but his dad had persisted. Three months later, they were married, and now, nearly forty years on, they were still blissfully in love. If persistence had worked for his father, Will was sure it could work for him. However, he couldn't keep presuming on Mrs. C.'s generosity. He needed to find a real job—a paying job—one the judge would respect.

"I'll pay for any damage," Frank said as he walked into the front of the shop with Louella in tow, a sullen expression on her face and her tutu torn to shreds.

"Just. *Get. Out!*" Mrs. C. yelled, picking up the lilies and hurling them at Frank. "And take these with you!" Mumbling under her breath, she went to survey the damage to her home.

Will glanced from Frank to Mrs. C.'s apartment doorway and then back again at Frank.

Frank shook his head. "I guess I left my run on Edna's affections too late."

Will didn't want to point out the obvious—he was around forty years too late. Still, where there was life, there was hope. "Let me talk to her. I think your romantic gesture was a mite too overwhelming for a woman of Mrs. C.'s, ah, *independence.*" He was going to say *age,* but thought better of it. If Frank was feeling his oats, then Will didn't want to go reminding either of them they were getting old.

"You'd do that for me, boy?" Frank pulled a cigar from his pocket, stuck it in his mouth and chewed on it.

"Where true love's concerned, I'd walk to the ends of the earth. On hot coals."

Frank nodded. "That you would, boy. That you would." He shot another forlorn glance toward the rear of the shop. "You let me know if there's anything I can do for you."

Will slapped his shoulder. "No problem, Mr. F." He hunkered down to talk to Louella. "Now, Lou, you've got to promise me you'll behave yourself. You've gone and upset Mrs. C. and spoiled your daddy's chances of a hot date tonight. Understand?"

The pig snorted and pushed her snout in Will's face.

Will wiped his face with his sleeve and stood. "Can I suggest next time you come visiting, you leave Lou in the car?"

Frank frowned, as though that hadn't occurred to him. "Excellent idea, boy. She was only jealous. Usually she's a good girl."

"Maybe she needs a four-legged companion," he said, thinking a certain dog of Miss P.'s would be perfect.

"I ain't gettin' another pig. Lou doesn't like other pigs. She gets real jealous and tears the place up. Much worse than this." He started to tidy up.

"I'll take care of that," Will said. "Your best strategy right now is to get out of here. I'll sweet-talk Mrs. C., sing your praises, and I'll tell you when the coast is clear for another visit. Okay?"

Frank slowly contemplated his suggestion. No wonder a live wire like Edna Carmichael had slipped through the older man's fingers all those years ago.

"If that's what you figure, Lou and I'll be gettin' along." He peeled off another two fifties and put them on the counter. "To pay for damages," he explained, then shoved a wad of cash into the donation tin. "For the buildings. Maybe it'd be better if Edna opened that bank account herself."

"To be fair and honest, it'll need two signatories, and considering you're our major donor so far, you should be one of them," Will assured him, determined to get Frank and Mrs. C. back on friendlier terms. When he looked doubtful about agreeing to be a signatory, Will laid a comforting hand on the older man's shoulder. "Let me talk to her. When she sees what a philanthropist you are, she'll change her opinion of you."

"A filla-what?"

"Philanthropist," Will explained patiently. "It means an immensely generous person. Someone who's public-spirited and charitable."

Frank's chest expanded with pride and he peeled off another wad of cash and stuck it in the tin. Large-denomination notes bulged out the top. Who knew owning a rock quarry was so profitable? Will decided the current trend of cladding new homes in local stone probably accounted for much of Frank's fortune.

"I'm organizing a fundraising barbecue at the ranch for the weekend after next," he said.

"It's winter."

"Exactly. Perfect time for a barbecue." Will rubbed his stomach. "Man, I can taste that brisket right now."

Frank was almost salivating. "Hey, great! D'you think your folks'll mind?"

"Nah. You know how Mom loves entertaining. We can hold it in the machinery barn and have a dance afterward." Will leaned toward Frank and whispered, "Maybe some slow dancing, Frank. I'm sure Mrs. C. would love to slow dance with you."

The older man's face lit up. "Anything you need, you call me."

Will saw Frank and Louella out, picked up the donation tin and went through to Mrs. C.'s home at the rear of her shop to ask if he could move into her upstairs apartment that evening.

Meanwhile, he was late for walking Miss P.'s boys. He'd have to leave sweet-talking Mrs. C. on Frank's behalf till later. Much later, because he needed to see the mayor before the close of business, then go out to the ranch and run his fundraising idea past his folks. He'd take his mom flowers.

WILL O'MALLEY! Becky fumed as she strode back to the courthouse. She'd popped out to see the florist to ask her to stop sending the flowers, but instead had found the man who'd been haunting her dreams sprawled on the floor covered in gerberas and with that blasted pig licking his grinning face! She was so furious she wanted to scream.

Why was it that everywhere she went in this town that man was there? And if she wasn't running into him unexpectedly, she was being assailed by dozens of roses with handwritten cards signed "Your secret admirer." As if she didn't know who *that* was! She was tempted to throw them away, but that would be too wasteful. She simply couldn't throw perfectly good flowers in the trash. No matter who'd sent them. So she'd filled the courthouse with them instead.

A small part of her enjoyed being wooed with flowers. It was a crying shame the man in question didn't have a job she could respect.

In spite of his failings, something about Will O'Malley appealed to her on an elemental level and Becky was damned if she could figure out why.

Chapter Five

Will paid the mayor a visit. Garrett Henderson had never liked Will and made it clear what he thought of his campaign to save the buildings.

He didn't rise to shake Will's proffered hand and things went downhill from there. He placed his size-seven Italian leather shoes on his expensive desk, leaned back in his chair and said, "When are you leaving town?"

Will mused that, for someone so large, the mayor had very small feet. "I'm not."

Mayor Henderson pulled his feet from the desk and leaned forward menacingly. "Yeah, you are."

"Excuse me?"

"You're not gonna stay, O'Malley. Everyone around here knows you never finish anything."

Will was unmoved. "Everyone?"

"Everyone who counts."

Everyone being the owners of the development company… Will had done some research on the directors. None of them were registered as voters within the county or the town. Except the mayor. "Everyone who counts to *me,*" Will said, "is fully behind saving those buildings. I'll stay as long as I'm needed. And then I might stay a bit longer. Maybe forever."

The mayor put his feet back up on the desk, tapped his

fingers together over the expanse of his belly and said, "I run this town, sonny. And don't you forget it."

"I think you're forgetting you run this town along with the council. And you'll only be doing it while you're in office."

"Which I will be for a very long time."

"Elections are coming up next year. Maybe I'll run against you."

That had the mayor sitting up and dropping his feet back on the floor with a thud. "The *hell* you will!"

Will remained unmoved by the mayor's threatening demeanor. "Keep giving your support to the development company and you'll lose your job."

"Not to you!"

Will shrugged and stood. He'd accomplished what he'd come for. He'd rattled the mayor, hinted he wasn't invincible. Not that the man's ego would concede that yet, but Will would let him sleep on it some. "Maybe. Or maybe to someone else. Come on out to the ranch next weekend and see how much support there is for saving those buildings."

He gave the mayor a casual salute and stalked out, hoping the man would back down and he'd never have to run for his job.

AFTER THAT, WILL BORROWED Matt's SUV, piled Miss P.'s dogs into it and took a ride out to the ranch.

While the dogs explored the house or relaxed on the comfortably worn furniture, Will told his parents about his plans for the fundraiser. Ever supportive, they made several helpful suggestions.

Luke was the fly in the ointment. He started off grumbling about too many people scaring his horses. Then he wanted to know where Will intended to put all the machinery from the barn he'd earmarked for dancing. "And where are you proposing to park all the cars?" Luke demanded. "Assuming anyone would be crazy enough to go to a barbecue in the middle of winter!"

For days, Will had rehearsed his answers to the various

scenarios Luke would be likely to raise and object to. Knowing his brother well and practicing paid off when Luke finally relented—after Will promised that everything would be returned to its usual order the day after the barbecue.

Since his brother was in a receptive mood, Will broached the subject of Luke seeing his way clear to adopting Edward, claiming he'd be excellent for rounding up sheep.

"We don't run sheep," Luke said.

"Well, I know that! He'll come in handy when you get some to keep him occupied."

Luke rolled his eyes. "Wait a minute. You're saying I should take this mutt off your hands—" he indicated Edward snoring at Will's feet "—and in addition, I should buy some sheep to keep him company?"

"Only a couple hundred head. Just enough to make him feel useful. Edward would appreciate it."

Luke shook his head. "What am I going to do with a brother like you?" he asked, grinning.

"Humor me?"

"I've been doing that all your life." He reached down and scratched Edward behind the ears. The dog responded with a louder snore. "Give me a week or so to think on it. And if he gets up to any mischief, I'll shoot him. Okay?"

"Yeah, sure," Will agreed, knowing full well his brother couldn't shoot straight and, within days, Luke's daughters would have Edward sleeping on their beds. He'd been joking about Luke buying the sheep. He was sure if Edward ever saw a real sheep he'd run away in fright.

Back at Miss P.'s, he outlined his plans for the fundraiser and told her about his meeting with the mayor.

"Oh, he's such a nasty man!" she said. "This town has done nothing but go downhill since he took office." Her face wrinkled even more as she frowned, then her eyes lit up and she clapped her hands. "Oh, I've just had a wonderful idea!"

Will grinned. Miss P. might be pushing ninety, but she had more enthusiasm than most teenagers. "I'm all ears."

She bustled out of the room and came back with a large art pad. She opened the pad and started to sketch.

BECKY'S FRUSTRATION OVER not finding a suitable caregiver for Nicolas during the upcoming holidays was evident when she dropped and broke three dishes as she cleaned up the kitchen after dinner.

All she wanted was someone to care for Nicolas in the afternoons, supervise his homework and make his dinner. Was that really asking too much? He might be in fifth grade but he was only eight, so too young to be left to his own devices. She was prepared to pay double the going rate, but so far none of the applicants were remotely suitable. Should she set her standards a little lower in order to get someone? Anyone?

"*No!*" she muttered as she opened the fridge and poured a small glass of wine to calm her nerves. Taking it to the living room, she curled up on the sofa. Nicolas deserved to have someone who cared about him—or at least knew how to care for a child. She'd devoted several lunch hours to interviewing candidates, and now she was getting desperate. The Christmas holiday was looming and Nicolas had told her tearfully that he didn't want to go to the program organized by the town, saying the bullies from school went there, too.

She rubbed her forehead. The fact that Nicolas was being bullied at school preyed on her mind. Coming to a small town, she'd thought all of that would be behind them, but it had reared its ugly head on several occasions. She'd spoken to Nicolas's teacher and the woman had reiterated that the school had a zero tolerance policy toward bullying and assured Becky she'd dealt with the perpetrator.

But Becky wasn't so sure. Nicolas seemed withdrawn and his tearful outburst tonight over attending the town's holiday program only worsened her fears that the bullying had continued. She'd tried to get him to talk about it, but he'd clammed up and gone to bed early. She'd have to make time to discuss it some more, but not when he was tired and overwrought.

She scanned the list of applicants she'd interviewed for the job. But reviewing the list caused her even more stress.

There were a number of questions she asked potential care-givers, to confirm that they were of the moral fiber and intel-lectual capacities she desired in her employees.

Frank Farquar's great-niece, Ellie, was one of the appli-cants. But when questioned about the types of movies she enjoyed, the teen had recounted a list of the most frightening and diabolically violent movie titles Becky had ever heard of. Ellie was a definite nonstarter. So was the woman addicted to soap operas and another addicted to both caffeine and tran-quilizers. Grandmotherly Virginia Smith had seemed prom-ising, until Becky discovered she was illiterate. The kindly woman had difficulty reading the simple list of duties Becky handed her. What hope did she have of helping Nicolas with his homework?

Many more interviews had taken up Becky's precious spare time and she groaned at the memory of the ways each and every applicant had proved unsuitable.

She took a deep breath to try to relax, but the scent of roses filled her lungs.

Will O'Malley! She couldn't seem to escape the man, even in her own home. And his name was on the register for tomor-row's hearings....

She tucked her feet beneath her and sipped her wine. What would he be up to tomorrow? And would he have the audacity to ask her out again?

WILL AND MISS PATTERSON worked into the night designing a poster for SOB. Miss P. created a watercolor painting of the mountains, with the town and its Victorian buildings in the foreground. While the painting dried, she and Will shared a pizza at her kitchen table.

"You're a very talented artist," he said, indicating the beau-tiful paintings of town scenes hanging around her house. "I hope I'm going to score a Miss P. original when I marry the judge."

Miss P. never sold her paintings, only gave them as gifts. They were a much-prized wedding present and many homes in the county had at least one Florence Patterson watercolor adorning their walls.

She patted his hand. "You can be sure of getting more than one, dear." Tonight she was as animated as a kid with an exciting project. "I'm so happy you like the poster idea. I was wondering how I could contribute to the cause," she said and bit into a slice of pizza. Her eyes widened. "My, this stuff is wonderful! I should eat it more often."

He laughed. Miss P. was another of Spruce Lake's living treasures. "You don't think being part of a human chain was enough of a contribution?"

She waved her hands dismissively. "Anyone can be part of a human chain, but not everyone can paint. I don't know why I didn't suggest this before." She frowned. "Do you think people would mind hanging the posters in their stores?"

Will covered her wrinkled hand. "I can't imagine anyone would object. The poster is lovely and so reminiscent of the town."

When the paint had dried, she'd written Save Our Buildings at the bottom of the poster.

It was nearly midnight when the task was finished.

"Now, I know you've got a court hearing in the morning, dear," she said. "So you run along and get some sleep and I'll go to the print shop first thing and have them copy this. By the time court opens, the town will be plastered with them!"

Will chuckled at her enthusiasm. "Don't forget, Mrs. C. has plenty of funds to pay for printing costs. Do you want me to come by and help put them up?"

"No, dear, you have enough on your plate with the hearing tomor— Oh! I mean, today," she corrected herself after checking her clock. "My neighbors have been wanting to help, so I'll send them all out with posters to the businesses on Main Street and beyond."

Will whistled as he strolled home and mused that it was people like Miss P. who made living in Spruce Lake special.

Exhausted, he tumbled into bed and dreamed of the house he'd build on his land. In his dream, Judge Becky was standing in the doorway, welcoming him home….

Chapter Six

Court seemed to drag on forever the next morning until at last Will O'Malley's name was called. A pleasant warmth suffused Becky when she glanced up to find him standing in front of her.

Devastating, was the only word that could describe how he looked *and* his effect on her peace of mind. He'd trimmed his hair and was wearing...a tie. A neatly pressed navy-blue shirt molded to his broad chest and muscled arms. The dark shirt accentuated his tanned face. Becky swallowed. He looked...magnificent. And masculine. And unbelievably sexy. If Will O'Malley asked her out now, she wasn't sure of her resolve to turn him down.

She'd spent a good part of the night remembering how wonderful his arms had felt around her. And then been preoccupied thinking of those strong arms at breakfast and had burned the toast—twice.

Get a grip! she lectured herself sternly. *This guy is a rogue and a heartbreaker and you don't want that.*

"Good morning, Your Honor," he said without his characteristic smile. He handed some papers to the bailiff, who passed them to Becky.

"This is a petition asking you to grant an injunction stopping the demolition of the buildings situated on Main Street," he said as Becky scanned the document.

He explained his reasons for seeking the injunction. He'd certainly done his research.

"Thank you, Mr. O'Malley," she said, then addressed the lawyers for the development company, lined up like tin soldiers. Five highly qualified lawyers against a lone petitioner. It didn't seem fair. "What do you have to say for yourselves?"

The Denver-based lawyers, led by Jason Whitby, wore smirks of derision, as though they believed "might was right" and they'd prevail in this small community.

Perhaps "might" ruled in the city, Becky reflected, but in a town like this, passion held a lot of sway. Judging by the size of the audience there was a great deal of passion in Spruce Lake. Also present were several reporters from Denver. It gave her a sense of satisfaction to know the campaign—and indeed the plight of many small towns attempting to maintain their unique character in the face of rampant development—was being taken to the city. The audience started to boo the lawyers for the development company as Jason Whitby began to speak.

Becky banged her gavel to restore order. "Silence!" she said. "Please remain quiet while the development company presents its case."

"They don't have a case. This is our town and we don't want them here!" Frank Farquar bellowed. His statement was accompanied by wolf whistles.

"Mr. Farquar, please leave the court," Becky said in her sternest tone. "And take your pig with you."

Louella snorted at her. Frank Farquar didn't budge. The Denver Five, as Becky had named them, rolled their eyes and snickered among themselves.

Will O'Malley turned to the audience and said, "Frank, everyone, please. This won't help our cause. You have to let the judge hear the other side."

Becky was taken aback when the audience immediately quieted and, with a nod of apology in her direction, Frank Farquar left with his pig at his heels.

She returned her attention to the Denver Five nudging one another like schoolboys, probably sharing a joke regarding her inability to control her courtroom without help. "You have something amusing you'd like to tell us, Mr. Whitby?" she asked.

"No, Your Honor," he shot back, trying to straighten his face and failing. Becky decided she hated him. He was making fun of her court. Making fun of the people of Spruce Lake who had a genuine love of their town. Okay, so they weren't the most sophisticated people in the world and no one brought their pigs to court in Denver, but Becky was beginning to realize that such eccentric behavior was part of the charm of Spruce Lake.

The only reason the Denver Five were here was because of money. Greed. The only reason the Mountain Resorts Development Company was in town was to make money. More greed. It made her angry.

In the past few days, Becky had inspected the buildings—not that she was any sort of expert—but if the posters supporting SOB, displayed in every store on Main Street this morning, were any indication of public sentiment, then this was a matter of vital importance to the town. Will O'Malley was correct, there'd been little or no public input into the fate of the buildings and that disturbed her.

She'd discovered the structures were a mix of former commercial and residential premises. Many were more than a century old and been vacant for decades, apart from a couple that were being used for storage. One was the former livery stables; another, the home of a freed black slave. There was a Mason's hall and an old chophouse that had served the miners, a Methodist church and even a former bordello. A half-dozen crumbling homes and a row of old shops completed the site.

As she'd wandered around the derelict buildings she'd felt an…atmosphere, as though beneath their shabby facades, each had a story to tell. Those stories shouldn't end in a pile of rubble.

The buildings would need a considerable amount of capital to make them habitable; however, they were worth preserving. She was happy to grant the injunction so they could try to find a solution.

Becky turned back to the lawyers who were still snickering. "Do you have anything to say?" she demanded.

Misreading her question, they sent back a collective, "No, Your Honor."

"Good," she said and picked up the injunction papers. "Mr. O'Malley, you've presented a most persuasive argument. On those grounds, and taking into consideration the support of the local community, plus the fact that counsel for the development company has nothing to say on the issue..."

Becky could hear rumblings of disagreement from the Denver lawyers, but ignored them. "I'm of the opinion a moratorium is warranted to prevent the demolition of the buildings while a satisfactory outcome for all parties is negotiated. I'm therefore granting an injunction for thirty days."

"But Your Honor," Jason Whitby protested. "You haven't heard our side."

Becky looked at him over her glasses. It was well past time to put this pack of ambulance chasers in their place. "Excuse me, *sir,* but less than thirty seconds ago I asked if you had anything to say and you *all* assured me you didn't."

"We were... We thought..." Jason Whitby glanced at his colleagues for support. They remained mute.

Becky enjoyed seeing "groupthink" in action. Particularly when it backfired and gave the advantage to the underdog. She wished she could be a fly on the wall when the Denver Five explained to their clients how they'd messed up in court this morning. It might've been arbitrary of her to cut him off, but that was her prerogative. She'd already decided the appellants had a strong enough case for granting the injunction. *Let that be a lesson to them for making fun of Spruce Lake!* she thought, surprising herself with her passion.

Jason Whitby tried again.

"You haven't allowed us to present our client's case, Your Honor."

Becky pinned him with a glare. "You don't need to," she said. "I want cool heads to prevail in this matter. The protest group has the right to try to find a solution. Your client won't suffer if they have to wait another thirty days. However, the demolition of those buildings will have a lasting and possibly devastating effect on this town." She signed the papers granting the injunction and returned them to Will O'Malley via the bailiff.

"Thank you, Your Honor," he said, then turned to the audience with the papers clenched in his fist. The courtroom erupted in loud cheers, accompanied by a great deal of backslapping.

Becky let them celebrate, wondering how the Denver papers would report this, then stood and walked out of the courtroom.

WILL SAT ON A STOOL at Rusty's Bar and Grill, nursing a beer, but he found it hard to join in the festivities. He'd woken at 3:00 a.m. in the grip of a nightmare about the avalanche. He'd felt moody and disoriented this morning. And he'd been afraid he might not be able to present SOB's case in court today without having a panic attack.

He'd had several nightmares since the avalanche. Mind-numbing, limb-numbing, heart-palpitating episodes that left him in a cold sweat and wondering if he'd function like a normal human being ever again. He'd worked hard on maintaining the facade of being in control, when deep down he thought he'd go to pieces—thought he'd mess up and let everyone down. They all had such blind faith in him. They'd won today. But what about next week? Next month? Next year when the development company had triumphed and the buildings were completely razed and replaced by an ugly mall and hundreds of condos?

Snap out of it! he told himself and took a long draft of beer, then choked as he was slapped on the back for what seemed the thousandth time that day.

"You've been uncharacteristically quiet," his brother Jack said. "What's up?"

Will shook his head. "Nothing much." He wasn't ready to reveal his fears to Jack, but then he reconsidered. Jack was the least judgmental of his brothers and always willing to lend an ear. He'd resigned from the priesthood a couple of years ago, giving little explanation to his family. He'd then trained as a carpenter and was developing a reputation for restoring Victorian homes. Jack worked long hours and, as far as Will was aware, hadn't dated since moving back to Spruce Lake.

"I'm trying to figure out our next move," Will said, pushing aside some tinsel that had fallen onto the bar. "I wish we had the funds to buy back the buildings."

"Fat chance, even with Frank donating wads of money every day."

That finally raised a smile from Will. Frank was making daily donations to the cause in order to see more of Mrs. C. She hadn't forgiven him for "the Louella Incident" yet, but she did offer a smile of encouragement whenever he stuffed money into the donation tin on her counter. Which, of course, encouraged Frank to donate more. They were also now both signatories to the SOB fundraising account.

In Will's opinion, it was only a matter of time until Mrs. C.'s heart thawed and she and Frank would be dating like teenagers again.

"Have you thought of having that ranch land of yours valued?" Jack asked. "You might be able to buy those buildings yourself."

Will rubbed his chin. "Matt said the same thing. But I paid a pittance for it and can't see how it could've increased all that much in value. You're talking millions of dollars."

"Anderson's old ranch got carved up into ten-acre housing lots last year and sold like hotcakes. You should look into it. It's a pretty valley. You might be surprised by what the land is worth—"

"Hey, Will!"

If Will had been standing, he would've been knocked flat by the force of Lloyd Wilmott's beefy paw landing in the middle of his back. The director of the ski patrol was a bear of a man standing over six foot six and built like a refrigerator. In spite of his size, he was hell on skis.

"I hear you're looking for a job. We need experienced people like you. Come and see me tomorrow."

During college, Will had been a member of the ski patrol. However, the strict discipline hadn't really worked for him.

He picked up a napkin to blot the sweat beading on his upper lip. This was exactly what he *didn't* need. Someone pressuring him to go up the mountains. And save people. He cleared his throat before saying, "Thanks for the offer, Lloyd, but I'm kind of tied up with saving the buildings."

Lloyd clapped him on the back again, nearly sending Will's beer flying. "Good man. Anything the ski patrol can do to raise public awareness, just let me know, okay?"

"Thanks, I appreciate it. To be honest, I always figured I didn't quite fit in with the ski patrol."

Lloyd frowned. "You're kidding, right? Okay, so you're a bit high-spirited, but you're also fearless. I knew if there was any sort of emergency, you were the guy we could depend on. That's why I want you back on the patrol. The pay's increased since you were doing it, too."

Lloyd tipped back his head and chugged a whole beer, then set the bottle on the counter. He wiped his hand across his mouth. "You've got the right stuff, buddy."

Will's spirits lifted at the heartfelt compliment. Maybe he should spend more time with Lloyd. The guy was doing wonders for his ego.

"This town could use more people like you," he said, clapping his big paw on Will's shoulder. "I've gotta get home, but I wanted to say I hope you're planning on staying for a while. The place always seems more lively with you around."

"If you took the job with the ski patrol, the judge might find you more attractive," Jack suggested when Lloyd left.

"It's not an option, so forget it," Will said, putting a stop to that line of conversation.

"The development company is going to make a killing pulling down those buildings and putting up a mall and condos. But what if you raised enough money by selling off your land to buy them back? I could renovate some of those old beauties to create shops with apartments above them, similar to Mrs. C.'s.

The houses would come back to life with some TLC. I'm not sure what you could do with the livery stables—maybe a museum. There are lots of possibilities. Plus there's some land that could be used for more housing, keeping the Victorian theme, of course."

Will replaced his beer on the bar and looked hard at Jack. "What are you saying?"

"Those buildings are brimming with the quaint charm that attracts people to Spruce Lake. Renovating them into a mix of retail and residential use would revive that end of town."

Will shook his head. "And Matt thinks *I'm* the dreamer in the family."

"What's gotten into you?" Jack demanded. "You're acting like a bear with a sore head. Where's your enthusiasm? Where's your vision?"

"If selling off my land could raise the capital to buy the buildings—provided the company's willing to sell them," Will hastened to add, "I still couldn't afford to renovate them. They'd sit derelict for another couple of decades." His shoulders slumped. "And then everyone would blame me for letting that part of town go even further downhill."

"Don't doubt yourself, Will, you can do this. I said I'd renovate the buildings. You know I'd do a great job and I'd enjoy the challenge. And you wouldn't have to pay me, just give me that old church as payment for services rendered." Jack smiled. "I like the idea of living in a converted church and I could make that little beauty into a decent home."

WILL WALKED BACK to Mrs. C.'s that night, his mind filled with ideas—*provided* he could buy back the old buildings. Jack's suggestion of renovating the site into shops, apartments and housing had inspired him. They'd retired to a booth and spent the next few hours drawing floor plans of shops and apartments on the paper tablecloth. Rusty kept up a steady supply as Jack's plans took shape. He was familiar with the size of the buildings and wasn't a half-bad artist, Will decided as his brother drafted proposals for the overall appearance of the buildings.

Restoring Main Street would necessitate Will's staying in town long-term and, for the first time in his life, the prospect didn't fill him with dread. Instead, he felt newly energized. Exhilarated.

As project manager, he'd have a worthwhile and fulfilling job. It might even make him attractive to the judge.

Chapter Seven

Nicolas McBride was terrified.

Johnny Cooper's immense bulk blocked his way out of the school grounds, preventing him from crossing the street to the recreation center.

"Goin' for your *therapy* session again?" Johnny sneered.

Nicolas fought the fear rising in his throat. "Yeah," he said, not making eye contact, hoping and praying the much bigger boy would leave him alone.

"When're you gonna to learn to walk, kid?"

"I don't know. But I'm trying," Nicolas said. Embarrassed about needing leg braces to help him walk properly, he didn't need Johnny pointing it out to everyone within hearing distance.

"Then try harder!" Johnny shouted and gave Nicolas a shove, sending him sprawling in the snow.

A few of the other kids laughed—friends of Johnny's, or kids who were scared of him, too. Nicolas fought back tears of humiliation as he tried to get to his feet, but it wasn't easy on the slippery, snow-covered ground.

None of the teachers were nearby and it didn't look as if any of the spectators were going to come to his aid. Nicolas swallowed bitter tears as he tried to regain his footing, but the other kids just laughed harder. They all despised him.

He'd been advanced two classes at Spruce Lake Elementary. His mother said being in a lower grade wasn't *intellectually challenging* enough for him, but Nicolas hated being with the bigger kids—especially kids like Johnny.

All he wanted was to be left alone. He *hated* being smart. It was no substitute for being physically normal. He didn't fit in. He ate lunch alone and spent most of his day trying to keep out of Johnny's way. He'd never again tell his mom he'd been bullied. Johnny had been really mad when he was hauled up to the principal's office and he'd been even meaner since.

"Get up, you dumb-ass weakling!" Johnny yelled, charging at Nicolas.

Nicolas braced himself, expecting a kick to the ribs, but someone yelled, "Get lost, Cooper, you jerk!"

Nicolas looked up into the face of an angel. "Come on," she said, offering her hand and helping him to his feet.

"Who's yer girlfriend?" Johnny sneered.

The girl released Nicolas's hand and said, "As if you don't know, you dumb bully! And in case any of your friends *don't* know," she said, surveying the group, "I'm Sasha O'Malley and this guy—" she drew a startled but grateful Nicolas toward her "—is a friend of mine. So don't mess with him, okay?"

The other kids backed off, but not Johnny. "You don't scare me," he scoffed.

"Then maybe *I* will!"

Another girl, a pint-size one, stood with her fists raised, lips pinched together in a grimace, eyes narrowed with challenge. Nicolas was scared of her, although she was at least six inches shorter than him.

"Don't waste your breath, Daisy," the older girl said. "Johnny Cooper's nothing but a bully." She turned her attention back to him. "I can't wait till you go to middle school, you rat. Maybe someone there'll beat *you* up, the way you like to beat up kids who're weaker than you."

Nicolas wasn't happy about being called "weaker," even if it was true. He wished the ground would open up.

"Well, *I'm* not weaker'n him!" the little girl yelled. She ran at Johnny and punched him in the jaw. Johnny went down and she leaped on him.

Then all hell broke loose. Sasha yelled, "Run!" at Nicolas while the little kid squabbled in the snow with Johnny. Despite her entreaties, Nicolas was glued to the spot, unsure what to do—help the little girl before Johnny got the upper hand and killed her, or run away as Sasha commanded. Although Johnny was twice her size, the little kid flipped him over and pinned him to the ground just like Nicolas had seen cowboys do to calves in the rodeo. She straddled Johnny's back, grabbed a fistful of his hair and pulled it back.

"Go! Now!" Sasha cried again, pushing Nicolas toward the school gate.

The rest of the other children had cleared off, standing a safer distance away. Nicolas still couldn't decide what to do, but the little kid and Sasha were giving him a chance to escape. So he took it, moving as fast he could across the road to the safety of the rec center before Johnny could push the little kid off and come after him.

Now, as he sat waiting for his therapy session, he felt cowardly for running away. He should've stayed and helped the girls—although he had no idea what help he would've been. They sure were brave. And the little one was *really* tough! He'd have to find them at school tomorrow and thank them.

He wouldn't tell his mom what had happened, otherwise she'd march right up to school and demand Johnny be punished. And then Johnny would punish *him!*

Nicolas had learned his lesson—keep quiet and pretend everything was all right, rather than speak up and make more trouble for himself.

WILL STROLLED INTO the Spruce Lake Recreation Center. Situated on the lakefront and across the street from the elementary school, it was an impressive indoor complex that served the county and consisted of a twenty-five-meter pool, hot tubs, a sauna, steam room, exercise facilities and squash courts. A hydrotherapy pool was separated from the main pool by full-length glass paneling.

Will waved at Jessie Sullivan, an old school friend and now a physical therapist, as she worked with a client in the hydro pool.

Since he couldn't even think about going skiing without provoking a panic attack, he'd decided that swimming would be the next best exercise. He dived in and concentrated on powering up and down the pool, lap after lap. By the start of the fifteenth lap, he was feeling the effects of the high altitude and lack of oxygen.

Cruising to a stop at the shallow end, Will lifted his head to catch his breath and found a pair of legs three inches from his nose. They were kid's legs and were encased in braces below the knees. Will glanced up and was met by appraising blue eyes.

"Hi. You're a good swimmer," the kid said.

"Thanks." Will caught his breath. Didn't want the kid thinking he wasn't fit. "Coming in?"

"I'm not allowed to swim in this pool."

Will looked from side to side. "Who says?" he asked and raised his fists. "I'll show 'em!"

The kid laughed. "You're funny."

"Why aren't you allowed in this pool?"

He made a face and said, "Mom says it's too dangerous. I'm only supposed to go in the hydro pool with Jessie. I do therapy with her."

That would explain the leg braces. "Jessie's a good therapist. Is she teaching you to swim?"

"Nah. We just do boring stuff. I'm not strong enough to swim freestyle."

The kid gazed longingly at the other swimmers as they did laps up and down the pool at a more leisurely—and more sensible—pace than Will had.

He sensed a vulnerability in the child and a yearning as he watched the swimmers. For Will, learning to swim had come as easily as breathing, but life had thrown this kid a curveball. "I'll teach you to swim if you want to give it a try," he said.

The kid's eyes lit up. "You mean it? Wow! You really mean it?"

Will admired his enthusiasm. "Sure. What's your name?"

"Nicolas." He thrust out his hand.

Will hauled himself out of the pool and shook the kid's hand. He was a cute kid. Red hair, freckles…leg braces.

Nicolas stared up at him. "You're real tall."

Will grabbed his towel and wiped the water from his face. "Nah, only about six-two. You'll be tall one day."

The kid gestured down at his leg braces. "I dunno."

"Swimmers are usually tall," Will said, not knowing if this was true, but it might cheer the boy up.

"Really? I want to be tall. And swim in a race," he said.

"If you wish for something hard enough, it'll come true," Will told him, thinking the kid might well end up learning to swim.

"I wish I had a dad." As if realizing that wasn't possible, the kid said, "I wish I could get a dog for Christmas."

Hell! Leg braces and no father. The kid had it rough.

"There you are!" Jessie said, joining them. "I see you've met an old school friend of mine, Nicolas."

"He's going to teach me how to swim."

Jessie glanced up at Will, her eyebrows raised. "Really? And when does he propose to do that?"

"When he gets his mom's permission."

"Good luck! She's extremely overprotective," she added in an undertone. "You'll need to produce documented evidence of certification as a swim instructor. Advanced level."

"A level-three ski instructor's certificate won't do?"

Jessie giggled. "Hardly!" She smiled at the kid. "Ready for your session, Nicolas?"

"Sure. Nice meeting you," he said to Will, then ambled with an awkward gait toward the hydrotherapy pool enclosure.

"What's his problem?" Will asked.

"Slight cerebral palsy. But he's smart as a whip and a great kid." She turned to Will. "That was sweet of you, offering to teach him to swim."

As Will observed the kid undoing his leg braces, he reflected that he'd had so many more opportunities in life than this little guy. "Maybe I'll teach him to ski, as well."

"Will O'Malley! Your reputation as a pied piper is well-deserved," she said. "Provided his mom agrees, I know Nicolas would love spending time with you. He's eight, and he doesn't have a dad, so there's no male role model in his life. I'll talk to his mom about your offer when I get the chance. I take him home after therapy," she explained, "but we don't usually have time to chat."

"No hurry. I'm pretty busy this week, organizing a fundraiser at the ranch. But next week I'm free." A thought occurred to him. "I'm getting some flyers for the barbecue printed up. I'll drop them over and leave one for Nick. Maybe he can get his mom to come along and I could ask her myself."

As he showered, Will wondered if the judge ever swam at the rec center. At least here she wouldn't find him flat on his back covered in Christmas trees or pig kisses.

"HOW WAS YOUR DAY, Mom?" Nicolas asked. "You look kinda frazzled."

Becky kicked off her shoes and flopped down on the sofa beside him. "Where did you learn a word like that?"

"School."

Becky smiled absently. Will O'Malley definitely made her feel more than a little *frazzled.* He made her feel hot and bothered. And after his antics this week outside the courthouse—and that kiss he'd managed to plant on her throat that still made her tremble at the memory—she was equal parts embarrassed, aroused *and* frazzled. The man's strangely taciturn behavior in court yesterday still had her puzzled, though.

"Flowers?" Nicolas sniffed the roses Becky had brought home with her from the courthouse. "Pooh! They stink."

Becky couldn't help smiling at his typically little-boy reaction. "They might stink to you, young man, but to a woman they smell beautiful."

"Who sent them? He must be rich."

Becky smiled to herself. No, he wasn't rich, far from it.... She caught herself, then frowned. What was she doing, letting herself daydream about a delinquent like Will O'Malley?

"What's up, Mom? Am I in trouble?"

Becky stretched out her arms. "No, sweetie. Come and give Mommy a hug and tell me about your day." She kissed the top of her son's red mop of hair as he curled up on the couch beside her.

But her mind kept wandering from Nicolas's animated description of his day at school—he'd made friends with a couple of girls—to Will O'Malley and the very flattering thought that he must have worked very hard to pay for the roses. She'd been much too abrupt with him in the florist's shop, but seeing him there, covered in flowers and that silly pig running amok, had unsettled her.

"And I'm gonna get swimming lessons. Proper ones."

Becky was pulled from her musings. "Swimming lessons?"

"Yeah, this really neat guy said he'd teach me to swim."

"He *what?*" Becky sat up in alarm. Exactly what was going on down at that pool?

"Chill out, Mom. He's a friend of Jessie's. They went to school together. He even said that if I get some training, I might be able to swim in races."

"And how does he know this?" Nicolas would never have the strength to swim races. It was a miracle he could even walk! "I don't want you talking to strangers. I've told you how dangerous it can be."

"But he's a friend of Jessie's. He's big and strong and everyone at the pool knows him." Nicolas crossed his arms and sighed. "Mom! Sometimes I don't think you listen to me."

"Of course I do, sweetie. I'm just tired and wasn't concentrating. I'm sorry." She sat up straighter and looked intently at her son. "I'm all ears."

"Okay." Nicolas drew in a breath. "You know how I've been writing to Santa and asking him for a puppy? For *three* years?"

Becky didn't like where this was going; she didn't have time enough for her son, let alone a dog. "Ye-es," she said cautiously.

He crossed his arms, his mouth set in a determined line Becky knew only too well.

"Well, I'm writing to him again this year, and if he doesn't bring me a puppy, then I'm not going to believe in him anymore!"

Chapter Eight

"I've found homes for Charles, Dermott and Edward," Will informed Miss Patterson the next evening. He scooped up another of her chocolate chip cookies before Edward could claim it. The sheepdog was sprawled across the sofa, and over Will's lap. Henri sat prissily on Miss P.'s lap, apparently following their conversation. Dermott chewed on a toy. Charles was fast asleep at Will's feet, while Dugald perched along the back of the sofa, watching Will eat, his wiry head turned in query as if to ask, *When do I get some?*

"Oh, you dear, dear, boy!" Miss P. said and clasped her hands to her chest. "Tell me, who wants to adopt my boys?"

He broke off a bit of cookie, picked out the chocolate chip, then fed the cookie to Dugald when Edward's attention was elsewhere. "Well…you know most of the folks at the Twilight Years, since you grew up with them."

"The Twilight Years?"

Will frowned. Maybe it was time Miss P. should consider moving there herself, seeing she was having trouble remembering things. "The retirement home out near the golf course," he prompted.

"I know what the Twilight Years is, dear. But I don't understand how anyone there can adopt Edward. They aren't allowed pets."

"No, they aren't. But I had a chat with the director, who was feeling kindly toward me because of the ironing, and I suggested Edward would make an excellent therapy dog."

"A therapy dog?"

"A dog that helps people who have disabilities or just cheers them up."

"I know what a therapy dog is, dear," she assured him with a grin. "But Edward's never been trained as one."

"Doesn't need it. His area of expertise is lying around doing nothing much. The residents enjoy petting him. That makes them feel good—cheers them up no end—and Edward likes it, too. It's a win-win situation all around."

Will had reconsidered moving Edward to the ranch. In doggy years, Edward was a senior citizen and would probably be worn out by three boisterous young girls even if he wasn't herding sheep. So this morning, Will had taken Edward to the dog-grooming parlor. Then he'd borrowed Matt's SUV. Matt had grumbled about Will's borrowing his vehicle yet again and pointed out that it was high time Will got wheels of his own. But once Will explained what he had in mind, Matt had handed over his keys and said, "Good luck."

After loading Edward into the SUV, he drove out to the Twilight Years, introduced the director to the dog and asked if it would be okay for Edward to visit with the residents while he did a few hours' ironing and snow shoveling. Impressed with Edward's grooming and how well he bonded with the residents, the director didn't need much convincing about the benefits of adopting the old dog for the Twilight Years.

"The residents are making rosters for walking him. He'll be in doggy heaven over there and they said you're welcome to visit any time you want."

Miss P. dabbed at her pale blue eyes. "Oh, what a wonderful home for Edward to go to. He *would* love it there. You're such a thoughtful boy, Will. Have another cookie."

He accepted one and broke off a bit—without chocolate chips—for Dugald. "They asked if I could bring Edward back first thing tomorrow." He chuckled and rubbed Edward's ears.

"Truth is, I had a hard time getting him away, but I figured I'd better bring him home to make sure you approved of them adopting him."

She clasped her wrinkled hands to her chest, her eyes filled with tears. "Of course I do, dear. And it would be lovely to visit him."

"Frank Farquar's agreed to take Charles. I suggested if Lou had a four-legged companion she might not get up to so much mischief. Frank's keen to win back Mrs. C. and knows that isn't going to happen while Lou's misbehaving."

She nodded sagely. "Louella is a dear pig, but she's awfully spoiled. I hope she doesn't get Charles into trouble, too."

Will could understand Miss P.'s concerns. Lou had caused havoc around town pretty much from the day Frank's cousin Hank had given him the runt of the litter. Frank had hand raised Louella and she'd imprinted him as her parent. Now fully grown, she was only half the size of normal pigs. Hence her ability to ride around in Frank's car, rather than being left at home where she couldn't cause as much damage. "He'd like to come by and collect Charles later this evening, if that's okay?"

More tears filled Miss P.'s eyes. Alarmed that the sudden departure of her beloved companions might be too much, Will hastened to add, "He's promised to bring Charles by to visit whenever you'd like."

Miss P. nodded her gratitude. "What about Dermott?" she sniffed.

"I met a young family from Boulder while I was walking the boys this afternoon and it was love at first sight. The kids adored him and it turns out the mom grew up with a setter. They can't wait to make him part of their family."

"They sound lovely." She hesitated. "Can I meet them first?"

"Absolutely. They insisted on meeting you, too. In fact—" he glanced at his watch "—they're coming by in a few minutes."

If all went well, Dermott's new family would collect him on their way back to Boulder on Sunday. They weren't permitted to keep dogs in their rental condo here in town. On future visits, they'd choose dog-friendly accommodations, but for now Dermott would need to stay with Miss P.

"My hair!" Miss P.'s hand flew to her unkempt gray bun.

"Looks lovely," Will assured her as the front doorbell rang and the dogs started a chorus of barking in various depths of voice.

Dermott was first at the door and as Will opened it, he jumped up on one of the children—a boy of seven. Far from being put off by the big dog's enthusiasm, the child giggled and hugged Dermott. "See, Mom! Dermott loves me the most!" he cried. Two more children, an older boy and a younger girl, pushed their way inside and hugged Dermott—or at least tried to as the big red dog jumped around excitedly, greeting his new family.

Will made the introductions and excused himself. He still had to find a home for Dugald. Until he'd accomplished that, he wouldn't consider his job done.

The judge had taken a liking to the little guy and vice versa. Maybe he should drop by the courthouse tomorrow....

THE FOLLOWING AFTERNOON, Will strolled down Main Street. Dermott loped along, dragging him forward on one side while Dugald and Henri, trotting as fast as their little legs would allow, were attached to his other hand. As of this morning, Edward had moved into the Twilight Years and Charles was now living with Frank and Louella.

Even with two fewer dogs in tow, the stroll took longer than usual. People greeted him with, "Keep up the good work, Will," and "I hear there's a barbecue coming up at the ranch. I'll be there!" or "Anything you need, Will, just ask."

With his eye on the courthouse door, Will gave Dermott's leash a gentle yank to slow him down. Yep, life was looking fine. He was astounded by all the support for Save Our Buildings. Donations were pouring in to the SOB fund. Frank Farquar, in what Will suspected was an effort to spend more time with Mrs. C., came into her shop every day to donate generously. Frank's contributions alone amounted to a sizeable sum. Will smiled at the vision of Frank stuffing bills into the tin on her counter.

"What are you grinning at?"

Startled out of his musings, Will flashed a grin of welcome at the judge. "I was thinking what a beautiful day it is," he said, indicating the sunny skies and snow-covered mountains—one of his favorite views from Main Street. "It could only be improved by you adopting wee Dugald."

The Scottie's bottom waggled at the expectation of some petting and kind words. "Hello, Dugald," she said and bent to pet him. His bottom waggled more frantically. "Where are the others?"

"Gone to good homes," he reported, smiling with satisfaction. "And I'm pretty sure you won't be seeing so much of Louella in your courtroom from now on."

Becky glanced up at that, her eyes bright with anticipation. "How so?"

"Frank's adopted Charles as a companion for Louella. Now that they're together, she won't have time to cause havoc wherever she ambles."

Becky raised an eyebrow. "I don't want to think about how unnatural that relationship is." After petting Henri and Dermott, she stood. "I hope what you say is true. It'll be a great relief not to constantly see that pig."

Will was transfixed by her green eyes. She wore a tiny frown that didn't, for once, seem to be directed at him. *What could the judge have to worry about?* he wondered, as Dermott wound behind her to Dugald and Henri on the other side.

"Oh!" Becky exclaimed as the big dog forced her and Will closer together.

"I think we've done this dance before," he said, grinning.

IT FELT WONDERFUL being pressed against him again. So deeply pleasurable, she had to fight the urge to place her cheek against his chest.

When Dermott tugged on the leash, pulling them closer, she

gave in and did just that, closing her eyes with pleasure at the feel of his soft chambray shirt against her cheek, the hardness of his chest muscles beneath it, his oh-so-wonderful masculine scent as she breathed in slowly…and sighed.

"Having fun?"

She blinked and looked up. He was smiling at her in a way that said he *knew* what she'd been thinking. Wanting to fume at him for catching her, she asked instead, "Are you?"

"Oh, yeah," he growled, the deep resonance of his voice making her want to lay her cheek against his chest again. As if reading her thoughts, he wrapped his arms around her and brought her into his warm embrace. "I was hoping I'd run into you," he admitted, and lowered his head to kiss her.

His warm lips covered hers with just the right amount of firmness. Enough that she could pull away if she wished, enough to let her know the next move was hers. Her gloved hands curled into the fabric of his shirt.

He deepened the kiss, his mouth opening over hers, his tongue testing, teasing. She'd dreamed of being kissed by Will O'Malley for too many nights. And this was far, far better than her dreams.

He shifted against her, making her all too aware of how their kiss was affecting him. Shocked, she stepped back. "Mr. O'Malley! What do you think you're doing?"

"Kissing you. Giving you what you want."

Awareness flamed her cheeks. He was right; it was precisely what she wanted—his strong arms around her, his warm lips teasing hers, the wondrous feeling of being held by someone… Someone so blatantly *masculine.* She shook her head to clear it. Every time she got near Will O'Malley, her brain went on holiday. And now a crowd of spectators had gathered, reminding her of the humiliation she'd recently experienced in the same situation. Except today she was tempted to ignore the spectators and let him kiss her some more.

"Why don't we do something about exploring this attraction we share?" he said.

"We do *not* share an attraction," she snapped, trying to regain control of the situation—and of herself.

His cocked brow spoke of his skepticism. "You're not going to try and tell me this is all one-sided, are you? Because I can assure you, your feelings for me are completely reciprocated."

She fixed him with a glare. "Get your hands off me," she said through clenched teeth.

"Okay, on one condition."

"If it has anything to do with kissing you or agreeing to date you, then forget it."

"Absolutely nothing to do with our love affair whatsoever," he said, but before she could interrupt, he said, "Agree to take Dugald. It'll set Miss P.'s heart at ease to know he's gone to a good home. Dugald McBride has a lovely ring, doesn't it?"

Becky sighed. He was incorrigible. Incorrigible and crazy and infinitely kindhearted. And extraordinarily persuasive. The little dog might be the perfect companion for Nicolas and resolve the Santa problem. "All right, I'll think about it."

He hugged her.

"You said you'd let me go," Becky said, her voice muffled against his chest.

He released her and moved a step away and Becky wished she hadn't protested so quickly.

As he unwound Dugald's leash, Becky was regretting her promise to consider adopting the dog. She didn't need emotional entanglements. She wasn't usually so impulsive. She was *never* impulsive! The man was clearly having a detrimental effect on her sanity.

"I said I'll *think* about it," she said before he could hand her the leash. Okay, so Dugald wasn't the much-requested puppy, but this friendly little dog would give Nicolas something to focus on, care about. Love. In spite of his mini-tantrum last night, when he'd said he wouldn't believe in Santa anymore, Becky was pretty sure Nicolas already knew the Truth about the man in the red suit.

She crouched down to talk to Dugald. "Do you want to

come and live with me?" she asked and rubbed his wiry-haired chin. Dugald's bottom wriggled and writhed with pleasure. She glanced up at Will. "I can't promise anything until I've checked to see if it's okay to keep a pet where we live."

She stood and brushed her hands on her coat. "If I can have a dog, I'll get in touch with Miss Patterson in the next few days and see what we can work out." She held up a hand. "Please, Mr. O'Malley. No more public displays of affection, if you don't mind. Goodbye."

She turned and stalked off down Main Street, leaving Will grinning from ear to ear.

Chapter Nine

Loud banging on his door woke Will from a nightmare.

Heart racing, he sat up, taking a moment to grasp where he was. His heart rate slowed when he realized he was in Mrs. C.'s apartment and not half-frozen and suffocating in an avalanche.

He stumbled to the door and yanked it open. Matt was there, wearing his ski suit and boots. "I've got the morning off. Let's go skiing," he said and, without waiting for an invitation, walked into the apartment.

Will's heart rate kicked up again. He did *not* want to go skiing. Not in this lifetime, anyway. "Want some coffee?" he asked, needing to stall, giving him time to make up an excuse for not skiing.

"You're kidding, right? I've only got this morning off."

"I…can't. Got some campaigning to do."

"At eight in the morning? Tell you what—we'll do some campaigning up on the slopes. I'll ride one chair and you can ride another. That way, we get to ski *and* campaign."

Will messed around making coffee. What could he say to that? Matt's suggestion made perfect sense. Except Will was *not* going up the mountain. "I can't, okay?"

"Oh, *please,* you're the guy who was always dressed and ready to ski before seven, even though the lifts don't open till eight. What's got into you?"

With an unsteady hand, Will poured the coffee into two mugs, spilling some of it.

Matt grabbed paper towels and mopped it up. "You haven't skied since you got home. What's up?"

"I've been busy doing my community service, campaigning, walking Miss P.'s dogs, helping Mrs. C. and…things. Plus, I've got to buy a car today, so I won't have time to ski."

"What a crock of excuses! This is me you're talking to. Since when has anything come between you and a pair of skis?"

"Since I decided to settle down and make a go of living in this town."

"Not buying it, buddy. Being part of this town means participating in winter activities, and that means skiing. What's really going on?"

Will wiped the perspiration from his upper lip with the back of his hand. He couldn't run away from this anymore. There was nothing else he could do; he'd have to admit the truth.

"I…quit the movies…because I nearly died in an avalanche."

"*What?* When?"

"A couple of months ago. I'm so spooked by it, I can't even face getting on the chairlift, let alone going to the top of a mountain I've been up a thousand times before."

Matt shook his head. "What happened?"

"We were filming over fifteen thousand feet high in the Chilean Andes. I was responsible for checking out the snow conditions, but I miscalculated, came off a cornice and the snow started to slide. I fell over four thousand feet down the mountain."

Matt emitted a soft whistle and said, "Thank God you're alive! But predicting avalanche danger isn't an exact science. How long were you buried?"

"They got me out that night." He'd been half-frozen by then, but it wasn't the cold that had terrified him, it was the sensation of slowly suffocating to death and wondering if he'd ever be found. "I kept remembering the statistics drummed into me when I worked on ski patrol—more than half the people buried in avalanches don't survive. I've been in dozens of avalanches and gotten out before—avalanches other skiers died in. But this one had my name on it from the moment I felt it move. If only I'd checked more carefully, I'd still have a career and still be able to face going up the mountains here."

"You're worried there might be an avalanche in Spruce Lake? You know that won't happen because the resort blasts potential danger spots every morning." As if hearing Matt's proclamation, several deep booms sounded from the mountains, signaling the ski patrol was at work. "It's not like a film set where they want deep, pristine snow on film."

He knew Matt was right. But the mountains had always been a living, breathing thing for Will. They spoke to him in ways other people couldn't understand. Since the avalanche, what the mountains had to say wasn't something Will wanted to hear.

"I don't expect you to understand, Matt, but the thought of going up there makes me sick to my stomach."

"So let's play around on the kiddie slopes to get your confidence back," Matt suggested.

"Right now, I'm not sure I can strap on skis without panicking. What if I never ski again? What use am I to anyone?"

Matt clapped him on the shoulder. "Hey. Don't be so hard on yourself. C'mon, you want to have a snowball fight?"

Matt was offering him a chance to get back on his skis in a nonthreatening environment. Will knew he'd be crazy not to at least give it a try. Plus, after vowing to teach Nicolas to ski, he couldn't let him down. "Okay, I'll try the kiddie slopes," he said. "But I'm not promising anything more."

BECKY TOOK AN EARLY LUNCH to follow up a lead for a caregiver for Nicolas and drove to the ski-ticket office at the base of the mountain. However, Sammy-Jo Parsons wasn't available for the upcoming Christmas vacation period as she'd be working full-time at the office. Becky headed back to her car, even more desperate to find someone who could look after Nicolas on an ongoing basis. No…she was more than desperate, she was becoming frantic.

In an attempt to calm her frayed nerves, she concentrated on the beauty of the day. The sun was shining, the air was clear, the mountains majestic. There could be no prettier place in the world on a day like this.

Then she saw the O'Malley brothers horsing around in the snow. On the *children's* slopes.

They were laughing like kids. Will O'Malley was making a snowball. But unlike the wet snow back east, the Rocky Mountain snow was so dry and powdery it was nearly impossible to form into a good snowball.

He hurled his missile at Matt, hitting him in the face, but the snowball crumbled like talc. Matt tackled him to the ground and the pair wrestled in the snow while the ski-school children cheered them on.

It must be nice having a sibling you could horse around with like that, she reflected. Although their personalities were very different, she suspected the brothers' upbringing had forged a bond that could never be broken.

Family. Becky hadn't spoken to her parents since the day she'd left their rented double-wide trailer in some nondescript town—like so many of the other nondescript towns they'd lived in over the years. With only a tattered suitcase packed with equally tattered clothes, she'd hitchhiked all the way to Atlanta.

"Look out!"

A snowball hit the side of her face and the pulverized snow sifted down underneath the collar of her coat and shirt. She looked over at the culprit. *Will O'Malley!* Damn that man.

"Sorry, Your Honor," he said as strode up to her. "I tried to warn you when that chickensh—er, brother of mine ducked instead of taking my supersnowball like a man. Are you okay?"

Becky dusted the snow from her clothes, cursing herself for not wearing a scarf and not buttoning her coat for the short walk back to her car. The snow filtered down inside her shirt and was now melting against her bare skin, chilling her. She resisted the urge to shiver.

"Get away!" Becky batted his hands aside as he attempted to help her brush away the snow around her collar. Then she noticed his gaze falling to her breasts.

He swallowed.

She glanced down.

Her shirt had turned nearly see-through from the melted snow. Her lacy black bra was clearly outlined beneath the fabric. She pulled her coat across her chest and closed the top button. Unfortunately, that only forced the cold snow against her bare skin. This time she did shiver. She glanced up at Will O'Malley again. His gaze was still fixed on her chest. She cleared her throat.

"Sorry, Your Honor," he said and raised his eyes to her face. "It's been a long—I mean…ah, hell!" he said and looked away. If she wasn't mistaken, his cheeks were flaming.

That was interesting. Will O'Malley lost for words *and* blushing!

His brother joined them. "I'm sorry, Judge. I shouldn't have ducked. Will's snowballs can pack a punch."

"I'm fine," she assured him. "You seemed to be enjoying yourselves."

"It's been a while since we've played in the snow like that," Will said, smiling broadly. A couple of the children who'd been enjoying their antics came over.

"Are you Will O'Malley?" one of them asked.

"Yeah. What can I do for you?"

The kids crowded closer. "The ski-movie star?"

"Ah, yeah," he agreed—with little eagerness, she noted.

"Can I have your autograph?" they all asked at once.

"I don't have a pen."

Matt produced one from inside his ski jacket and handed it over.

"I don't have paper, either."

More children joined the crowd. Matt handed over a note-pad. Even off duty the guy was organized to a tee.

"Thanks," Will O'Malley told his brother without enthusiasm. He seemed embarrassed by the attention.

Matt drew Becky away from the excited children so she wouldn't be elbowed by them. Some held up cell phones and snapped pictures of themselves with their hero.

"I didn't realize your brother's fame was so, er, widespread," she said.

"We don't have many celebrities in town," Matt explained and looked fondly at his brother as he posed for photos. "You can see why he's known as the pied piper of Spruce Lake. Kids love him. Dogs, too."

Touched by the attention he bestowed on the children, she said, "You were right. He *is* kind, to animals, the elderly and children."

Matt laughed and said, "You gave me such a disbelieving look that day in court."

She shrugged in apology and he asked, "Do you ski?"

"Definitely *not.* My one and only attempt resulted in me upside down among the trees lining the ski run."

"That shouldn't have happened during class."

"I wasn't in a class. My college *friends* convinced me I didn't need to waste money on lessons. The experience was so mortifying, I spent the rest of the vacation curled up in front of the fire with a book."

"Any time you want to learn properly, give me a call," Will said as he joined them.

"Thanks for your generous offer, but I lack the courage to try again."

"I thought you said nothing scares you, Your Honor?"

"I don't *care* to try again," she said, irritated he'd called her on it and held up her hands as he began to speak. "Forget it. I won't be taking you up on it."

"Aw, Judge. I'm only trying to show you what an upstanding citizen I am."

Becky was almost tempted to relent. It did look like fun....

"Come to dinner with me tonight?"

"You don't give up, do you? My answer is still no."

"No to dinner? Or to me? We can eat anywhere you'd like." He wriggled his eyebrows suggestively. "Your place or mine."

She grinned, flattered despite herself. "No, Mr. O'Malley. No, no, no." Becky got into her car and lowered the window. "However, I would like to thank you very much for all the flowers. But may I make a request?"

"Anything!"

"I've asked you once and now I'm telling you. *Please don't send any more!*"

She started her car and drove off, leaving Will and Matt staring after her.

"She smiled at me. That's a good sign," Will said pointedly, knowing exactly what his brother was going to say.

"Correction. She smiled at something you said." Matt glanced at his watch. "I'm on duty in two hours. Let's get changed and go buy you a vehicle. I'm done with you borrowing mine."

"HEY THERE, CHAMP!" Will waved to Nicolas as he arrived at the pool.

"Hello!" The boy waved back and walked over with his awkward gait.

Will eased himself out of the water and stepped onto the pool surround.

"Can you teach me to do that one of these days?" Nicolas asked, his eyes glowing with admiration.

"You keep up the therapy, Nick—can I call you Nick?" He smiled at the boy's vigorous assent. "Anyway, Nick, you could be doing it in no time." He picked up his towel and they walked to the hydro pool area and sat on the benches provided. "Let me help you with those," Will said and bent to unclip Nick's leg braces.

"You'll really teach me to swim?"

"Sure." Will helped him walk to the pool. "Maybe I can ask your mom at the fundraiser we're having at the ranch this weekend. You *were* planning on coming, weren't you?"

"I wouldn't miss it for anything!"

The kid was so darned enthusiastic. And, as Jessie had said, smart as a whip. He'd pulled a face when he'd told Will he was two grades ahead of the other kids his age. He'd also revealed that some of his classmates picked on him. Will's heart had gone out to the little guy. Nick would be an easy target for bullies. It made Will doubly determined to spend time with him, to try to build up his self-confidence so he wouldn't be such an obvious mark.

"Maybe we could start those swimming lessons during the holidays," Will said.

"I don't know if I can get to the pool. My mom is looking for an after-school and vacation caregiver for me, but she hasn't got anyone yet. The problem is, she expects everyone to be as good at everything as she is, so I don't think she's ever going to find anyone," he said and sighed like an old man.

Will fought to keep a straight face. The kid was eight going on eighty.

"I wish she could find someone who's fun to be with." His features brightened as he gazed up at Will. "Someone like you would be *perfect.*"

Jessie waded over to them. "Hey there, Nicolas. Will. You two are becoming friends, aren't you?"

Nick giggled and held out his hands to Jessie.

"You're doin' so well, buddy," Will told him. "You'll be swimming in no time."

Nicolas squealed with delight. "D'you really think so?"

"If only all my clients had such a positive attitude, my job would be a breeze," Jessie said, grasping Nick's hands. She eased him off the side of the pool and into the water.

"Will you be here when I'm done?" he called as he was towed down the pool.

"Sure, buddy."

Will watched Jessie taking him through his routine for a few minutes. The kid had spunk. He wanted to try everything, too, even though his physical disability precluded him from most sporting activities. Will believed the unbeatable combination of enthusiasm and determination would see Nick learn to swim—and ski. The ski boots would support his legs in a similar fashion to his leg braces, and if they didn't, Will was sure he'd be able to rig something that would work.

Of course, first he'd have to get over his stupid fear of going up the mountain and, second, he'd have to speak to Nick's mom. The little guy said she didn't like him doing anything too physical in case he got hurt. Will wondered why, if she was so protective, she wasn't at the pool every afternoon, supervising his therapy.

WILL MANAGED FIFTY LAPS without expiring, then joined Nick at the conclusion of his therapy session.

"Maybe you could apply for the job," Nick suggested as they sat together on the edge of the pool. "I don't want to go to the vacation program run by the town."

Will pulled his feet out of the pool and wrapped his arms around his knees. "Why not?"

"'Cause...the bullies will be there," he said, wiping his face with a corner of his towel and draping it around himself as if seeking protection.

"I'm sure the program's got good supervisors," Will said in an attempt to quell his anxiety.

"Yeah, right! Just like they've got good teachers who always see what the bullies are doing at school."

Will had never been bullied, thanks to having older brothers who'd looked out for him. But he was aware that bullies targeted kids who were smaller, physically weaker and unlikely to tell on them for fear of retribution. It wasn't Nick's fault he was so smart he was several years ahead of his age group. And it wasn't Nick's fault that he had a physical disability. But the combination would be irresistible to schoolyard thugs. Unfortunately, no amount of lecturing about ignoring the bullies was going to work for a kid like Nick, because they'd zero in on his physical disability and taunt him about it till they completely broke his spirit.

Unable to bear the fear in his eyes, Will put a comforting hand on Nick's thin shoulder. "You know," he said, "bullies are weak people who're trying to make other kids feel worse than they do—the bullies, I mean—about themselves. For instance, some kids come from really unhappy homes where bad things happen." Will couldn't tell how much Nick knew about domestic violence, so he hedged around the subject and said, "They're in situations where they have no power and they get very angry about that and want to lash out. But instead of lashing out at the person they're really angry with—usually because that person is much bigger than them—they take out their anger and frustrations on smaller kids. It gives them a feeling of power." Will shrugged. "It's screwed up, but it happens."

The kid gazed up at him with something akin to hero worship. "I guess that makes sense. But I wish it wasn't happening to me."

Unable to think of anything else to comfort him, Will said, "Me, too, buddy."

"I wish my mom could throw them in jail."

Will couldn't help smiling. "I doubt you can make citizen's arrests on bullies. But the idea has merit."

"My mom can throw anyone she wants to in jail."

And now the kid was fantasizing. Will let it slide. If it made Nick feel better to believe his mom could throw people in jail, then what was the harm in that?

They sat in silence for a while, watching the other swimmers. What was it with his mom that she couldn't come to the pool to see how he was doing? Will was going to give the woman a piece of his mind when he met her.

But, for now, he needed to lift the little guy's spirits. "Would you like me to apply for that job?"

Nick's eyes lit up like a Christmas tree, and he hugged Will around the neck so fiercely he was nearly strangling him. "Oh, *yes.* Yes, yes, *yes!* When?"

"How about at the fundraiser tomorrow?" he said, disentangling Nick's skinny arms so he could breathe. "Your mom will be in such a great mood after eating some of that barbecue, she'll think it's the best idea she ever heard."

"Yeah! She loves barbecue… She likes red wine, too."

Will made a mental note to ensure that they'd serve red wine. It would be good to get the job as Nick's caregiver. The judge would respect him if he had a paying job and might agree to go out with him. The flowers certainly hadn't worked. Will hadn't sent any more since her second request that he stop—and after Matt had sternly pointed out that Will's unwanted deliveries might be construed as stalking.

Will got to his feet. "I'd better head out, buddy. I've got some stuff to do before the barbecue. See you there, and don't forget to bring your mom, okay?"

Chapter Ten

Saturday was sunny and clear, a perfect high-country winter's day. Up before dawn, Will attended to final preparations and snowplowed the car parking area. Matt and Jack arrived to lend a hand. Will could barely wipe the smile off his face when both of them complimented him on his latent organizational skills.

By eleven, the temperature had climbed into the mid-thirties and a steady stream of vehicles was entering the gates of Two Elk. So much for Matt's doubting the success of a barbecue in the middle of winter.

The response from the community was overwhelming. Frank had hired the winners of the summer barbecue festival cook-off. Mrs. C. had organized several community groups to serve food and drinks. A mobile coffee van was dispensing hot chocolate and coffee of all varieties, while the Boy Scouts sold sheets of tickets to be exchanged for food and drink at the stalls. A local band had donated their time. The strains of their tuning up emanated from the barn.

With the beer wagon in place and the tempting aromas of barbecue, kettle corn and funnel cakes filling the air, it promised to be a very successful event.

Will watched fondly as Sasha helped direct cars to park, then raced back to report who'd just pulled in.

He ruffled her fair hair. "You're doing a great job, honey," he said and pointed back toward the parking area. "Better go catch those folks before they slip into the wrong spot."

"As if! Daisy's herding them with her bullwhip, so they don't stand a chance."

Will smiled at the sight of Daisy, bullwhip in hand. He could see her taking over the ranch from Luke one of these days.

"My girls behaving themselves?" Luke asked from behind him.

Will spun around. "Always do," he said and was about to suggest Luke view his children more positively, when his brother threw him for a loop by saying, "I didn't think you'd manage to pull this all together. You've impressed me."

He moved on, leaving Will openmouthed with shock at the biggest compliment Luke had paid anyone in a very long time. If ever.

Will purchased a sheet of tickets and handed over a couple for a plate of brisket. He surveyed the barbecue area filled with friends, neighbors, townsfolk and tourists enjoying the sunshine, talking, munching on corn or ribs, greeting old friends. It seemed half the county was at Two Elk.

He wandered toward the barn, where people boot scooted to the band's popular tunes. He'd join in later. Maybe when the judge got there.

"Uncle Will! Uncle Will!" He spun around to see Sash dragging another kid behind her. "This is my friend, Nicolas!"

"Hey, buddy!" Will high-fived the kid. "Glad you could make it."

"You know each other?" three female voices chimed in unison.

Daisy and Sash wore identical frowns of confusion. The judge, who'd now joined them, looked more bothered than confused.

"Sure. We met at the rec center. Howdy, Judge. Welcome to Two Elk."

"How do you know this man?" Becky asked Nick.

Wearing a smile from ear to ear, he clasped Will's hand. "I told you about Will. He's gonna teach me to swim."

The judge's eyes narrowed as she surveyed Will, then looked

pointedly at their joined hands. Will eased his hand from Nick's and said to the boy, "We were going to talk about that with your mom first, buddy." He turned to Becky. "How about you let me teach this little guy to swim?"

Will enjoyed watching the judge's features crease with consternation, figuring it wasn't often she got her feathers so ruffled. He'd finally worked out who Nick's mom was after he said he wished she'd put all the bullies in jail. Will knew every female cop in town and in the sheriff's department. The only other woman who could jail anyone had to be the judge.

And now he saw them together, their resemblance was unmistakable—red hair, freckles, cute smile, when the judge allowed herself one. Right now, she wasn't smiling.

Becky crooked her finger at him, indicating Will should follow her away from the children.

"Mr. O'Malley, I have no idea how you discovered my son does sessions at the hydrotherapy pool. And I especially don't appreciate you befriending him in order to get closer to me."

Will held up his hands. "Whoa there! You're right off track, Judge—"

"I want you to stay away from him!"

Stung by her vehemence and what she was intimating, he said, "You think I'd harm the little guy?"

"I would hope not, but an older man befriending a child is *not* appropriate!"

That did it. He'd had a gutful. He'd tried to be nice to her, welcome her into the community. Date her. But to suggest that meeting Nick at the pool had some sort of nefarious intent was going way too far. "You know, *Your Honor*—" Will put the emphasis on the words, since she obviously thought she was far above the rest of the folk of Spruce Lake, especially him "—I've had it with your attitude toward me."

He counted off on his fingers a few points for her to consider. "One, I met *Nick*," he said, shortening the child's name, figuring it would probably annoy her, "last week at the pool. Two, he said he wanted to learn to swim like me. Three, I offered to teach him, provided he got his mom's permission. Four, I didn't know *you* were his mom until yesterday. Five, and even if I'd known, I would still have liked him." He let that remark sink in before continuing. "He seemed lonely, desperate for friends. I'm sorry you think I'm an inappropriate friend. No one else in this town would think that, but you seem hell-bent on believing the worst of me—"

"The mayor—"

"Is a horse's rear end, intent on lining his pockets and destroying our town in the process. If you want to believe him, go ahead."

Will saw the bus bringing the residents of the Twilight Years. "If you'll excuse me, I have guests to greet." He turned away from Becky, called out, "Catch you later, buddy," to Nick and headed for the bus.

Will worked on keeping his temper in check as he strode toward it. What had he ever seen in the woman? She was crabby, judgmental and just plain *wrong* about him. Forcing his confrontation with the judge from his mind, Will greeted the residents of the retirement home. "Mr. Whittaker! Glad you could make it," he said, shaking the older gentleman's hand. "Miss Patterson, I see you hitched a ride. Hey, Sol, love the new hair."

Out of the corner of his eye, Will noticed Matt leaning against the barn, grinning at him. The jerk! Matt had known all along the judge was Nick's mom.

BECKY FUMED as she observed Will greeting the residents of the Twilight Years. How *dare* he speak to her like that?

"What were you guys talking about?"

She spun around. Nicolas had his arms crossed and was frowning.

"Why didn't you tell me you knew that man?" she countered.

"I told you about meeting Will at the pool last week."

"You didn't mention his name." If he had, she would've made the connection earlier.

"Yeah. I did. But you didn't seem all that interested in what I do at the pool."

Ouch! Nicolas had a point. She'd been so busy at work and preoccupied with finding a caregiver, she hadn't been paying attention. She had, however, let Nicolas and Deputy O'Malley talk her into coming to the fundraiser.

She glanced toward the barn. Matt O'Malley lounged against it, observing her and looking much too pleased with himself. Becky was tempted to—

"Grandma!"

"Daisy, darling, try to keep your voice below a roar," a tall, slender woman said as she approached them. Her fair hair was pulled back into a knot and her vivid blue eyes danced with love as she gently chided her granddaughter. "You're not out in the paddocks now, dear."

"Grammy, this is Nick, our friend from school."

"Good to meet you at last, Nick," the older woman said, extending her hand. "The girls talk about you all the time." She smiled at Becky. "Hello. I'm Sarah O'Malley."

Becky wanted to groan. Of course this would be Will's mother, since these girls, Sarah and Daisy, were his nieces. "I'm Judge McBride—ah, Becky," she corrected herself. "Nicolas talks about the girls a lot, too."

"Are you enjoying yourselves?" Sarah asked.

"We haven't been here very long," Becky admitted. "Can I buy you a coffee?" she asked, determined to make a friend of this woman who'd opened her home to so many people for a good cause.

Sarah rewarded her with a warm smile. "That would be lovely."

"Can I go and help the girls with parking?"

Becky looked at Nicolas. Would it be safe to let him wander around a parking lot? He could slip in the snow.

As if reading her mind, Sasha said, "He'll be fine with us, Judge McBride."

"You're welcome to call me Becky, if you like. You, too, Daisy. It was a pleasure to meet you both. I'm delighted to see Nicolas has such delightful friends."

The girls rewarded her with identical deep-dimpled smiles reminiscent of their uncle's.

"Thank you for saying that to them," Sarah said as they walked toward the coffee van. "I'm afraid they don't get enough compliments from their father. I'm always having to remind Luke about that."

Luke O'Malley had been pointed out to Becky as he drove through town one day. He seemed a rather grim man.

Becky ordered two lattes, then turned to Sarah. "How many sons do you have?" she asked, spotting the one who'd caused her the most distress, peeling an ear of barbecued corn for one of the ladies from the Twilight Years.

"Five." Sarah's gaze followed Becky's. "Will would make the most wonderful father. I wish he'd settle down," she sighed.

Becky didn't have anything to say to that, apart from perhaps mentioning that Sarah's son had barely left childhood himself. He was now engaged in a snowball fight with a group of teenagers. To change the subject, she said, "*Five* sons? Where does Matt fit in?"

Sarah grinned at the mention of the deputy sheriff. "Of course you'd know Matt! He's the second oldest and has always been the protective one. His wife was killed by a drunk driver several years ago and he's never gotten over it. I doubt he ever will."

"If the right woman comes along, perhaps he'll open his heart."

"You sound as though you speak from experience."

"Of a broken heart? Yes." Realizing she'd revealed more than she wanted, Becky said, "I've been divorced since Nicolas was a baby. I understand the need to protect one's heart." Again Becky realized she'd said more than she should. What was it about Sarah that had her spilling her guts? "Sorry, I didn't mean to get that personal."

With kindness in her eyes, Sarah said, "I hope you'll get to know me and trust me enough to tell more of your story some day, Becky. I sense you're a woman of immense depth and intelligence."

Becky smiled, touched by the compliment.

Sarah waved to someone in the crowd, but there were so many people now, Becky couldn't see who it was. "That's Luke," Sarah told her. "He's the oldest and runs the ranch and is Sash and Daisy's father. His other daughter, Celeste, is over there, taking a walk with her grandpa." She indicated a tall, graying man holding the hand of a toddler. Her smile showed her adoration for both man and child. "She's devoted to her grandpa and is the only child I know who prefers someone else to Will."

Becky needed to steer the conversation away from Will. "I've heard the name Jack O'Malley mentioned, too."

"Jack is number four. That's him talking to Miss Patterson. He was training to be a priest, but left the seminary."

Becky followed her gaze to the strikingly handsome man who was listening intently to the older woman. Becky tried to picture him in a cassock and wondered if he'd left because he was unable to keep his vow of celibacy.

"Jack's a patient listener and wonderful counselor. If you ever have a problem, he's the one to go to. He's very good at keeping secrets."

"As a priest should be," Becky said.

Sarah's smile softened. "He would've made a wonderful priest, but I'm very happy to have him back in the family fold. It didn't feel right not being able to pick up the phone and talk to him anytime I wanted. Or see him around the dinner table laughing with his brothers. I don't know if he'll ever marry. He was in love with a girl during high school, but she broke his heart."

"Broken hearts run in the O'Malley family?"

"I hope not. But when an O'Malley man falls for a woman, he falls hard. And if it doesn't work out, it takes a lot of courage to risk your heart again."

Becky liked this woman. Sarah loved her sons dearly and wanted to see them all happy. And married.

"Adam's the youngest," she said, bringing Becky back to the present. "He's a firefighter in Colorado Springs and unfortunately couldn't make it today. I hope you'll get to meet him sometime. I'm sure you'd like him. Adam's a lot like Matt."

"If he's anything like Matt, then I'd enjoy meeting him."

"You must come to dinner soon and meet the rest of my boys. I know Nick would hit it off with them."

Becky was astounded at the woman's generosity and, although accepting the invitation would mean she'd be spending time in Will O'Malley's company, she said, "That would be nice. Thank you."

She glanced over at the parking area, where Nicolas was helping direct vehicles. The girls were watching him carefully and she appreciated their attention. When he slipped on the snowy ground, Daisy matter-of-factly gave him her hand and hauled him to his feet. For a little girl, she was awfully strong and awfully loud, but Becky had warmed to the sisters instantly. They'd accepted Nicolas without staring at him rudely like so many children—and adults—did.

"May I ask what Nick's problem is?" Sarah inquired quietly. "I notice he has a little trouble walking."

"He was born with cerebral palsy. But he's very intelligent," she added quickly.

Sarah's brows went up at that. "You seem a little defensive."

Before she could respond, Sarah said, "Sash told me about a boy at school who was being bullied. She and Daisy went to his rescue. I'm assuming they meant Nick."

Becky tensed at her revelation. Nicolas had assured her he wasn't being bullied anymore! Why would he have lied to her?

"You didn't know?"

"He…he told me he'd made some friends. I thought everything was fine and the bullying had stopped."

"He'll be all right if Sash is close by. Or Daisy—that little girl never backs away from a fight. But Sash is in the grade below Nicolas, so she can't be around to watch over him all the time."

"You make her sound like his protector."

"Sash has always stood up for the underdog. She's so like

Matt was as a child." Sarah looked at her granddaughter with a loving smile, then turned to Becky again. "Would you consider putting Nicolas back a grade so he can cope better socially and get away from bullies like Johnny Cooper?"

"Of course not. He wouldn't be intellectually challenged if I did that," Becky answered a little harshly.

Sarah placed a calming hand on her arm. "The only way your little boy is being *challenged* at the moment is by trying to stay clear of Johnny's fists. That kid is nothing but trouble. There's not much the school can do about him."

"They could expel him."

"And where would he go? There aren't any other elementary schools in this town. He'll be going to middle school next year but, in the meantime, do you want Nick to have to deal with him on his own? And then have to face it all over again next year?"

Becky fought to keep her temper under control. "He won't be attending middle school here. When my term's up, we'll be returning to Denver."

"You're not staying in Spruce Lake?"

"Heavens, no! I'm only filling in for six months while Judge Stevens is on maternity leave. Nicolas has been accepted into a gifted school there starting in the fall semester. His education has been put on hold for too long."

"You think Spruce Lake is a backwater that's not worthy of you?" The woman's hurt and disappointment were palpable.

Becky sighed. "I'm sorry, I didn't mean it like that. But at a gifted school, Nicolas will be challenged intellectually to achieve his full potential. He's not doing that here. Not even two grades ahead of his age group."

"You believe graduating from high school so young is important? That the educational opportunities of living in a city outweigh unlimited fresh air and the freedom to move?"

How could someone like Sarah possibly understand? "Nicolas is not a physical person. Unlimited fresh air and room to move are wasted on him. His mind needs to be challenged and nurtured, and that's not happening here."

"I'm sorry you feel that way. I don't think any of my children suffered because they weren't exposed to constant intellectual stimulation. None of them graduated summa cum laude, but they were happy, contented teenagers with a wide circle of friends. They all attended college and have worthwhile careers."

Becky didn't see any point in continuing the discussion. Sarah O'Malley had a simplistic attitude to life and could never understand that a child like Nicolas was destined for great things, far beyond the limits of Spruce Lake, Colorado.

"I can see you don't agree with me, dear. But I'm speaking from experience. I wouldn't trade my family and my life here for anything. I've found a contentment in this place and among these people that I would never have found had I completed my doctorate at MIT."

It took a moment for Sarah's words to sink in. "You were in a doctorate program at MIT?" Becky asked in disbelief. "Why did you give it up?"

Sarah's blue eyes twinkled. "I fell in love."

"But—"

"All the degrees and scholarship and accolades in the world mean nothing unless you have inner peace. I found mine with Mac and I've never regretted my decision. Not once."

"But...you could've achieved so much more if you'd stayed and finished it."

Sarah shrugged. "So much more of what? Late nights spent poring over research and textbooks? Days taken up with examinations and the constant stress to achieve high marks? I was a driven child, Becky, the product of overachieving parents. I graduated from high school at fifteen and had two degrees by the age of twenty. But I wasn't truly happy. And I'd never been in love. Not until the day I saw MacKinley O'Malley at a college football game. Our eyes met as he pulled off his helmet and I knew he was The One."

Becky laughed. "That's a little melodramatic. And what's falling in love got to do with Nicolas? He's barely eight years old."

Sarah placed her hand on Becky's arm. "I'm trying to point

out there's more to life than excellent grades. Nicolas is smart enough. Putting him up several grades isn't going to improve his chances of getting into an Ivy League university if that's what you're after. Let him be a child, let him breathe and enjoy pursuits that aren't wholly intellectual. You'll have a much happier little boy."

The older woman's attention was drawn away as someone approached from behind Becky. "Darling! You must be pleased with the turnout."

"Sure am, Mom. You two getting acquainted?" Will O'Malley asked, and kissed his mother's cheek.

"More like your mother's telling me how to raise my son," Becky said without thinking. She bit her tongue and said, "I'm sorry, I…I'm not used to people telling me what to do with Nicolas. I've made all the decisions for him on my own and I'm not accustomed to other people sharing their opinions on how to raise him."

"You're doing a wonderful job, Becky," Sarah assured her. "He's a charming boy and my granddaughters dote on him." She indicated the children talking animatedly as they ate corn on the cob.

"Mom knows how to raise sons," Will said, hugging his mother to his side. "Just look at how well I turned out."

Sarah swatted his arm. "Let's not discuss your behavior of late. I only agreed to hold the barbecue here because I was so embarrassed by your antics and felt the O'Malleys needed to make amends."

Far from being castigated by his mother's remark, he grinned broadly.

"Why don't you give Becky a tour of the house?" she suggested. "I see some people I need to catch up with." She took Becky's hand. "It was a pleasure to meet you, and I do hope you'll take up my invitation to dinner sometime."

"Thank you, I'd like that," Becky said, then turned to Will, ready to make an excuse to avoid touring the house with him. But any sensible excuse fled as their eyes locked. There was something unfathomable in his dark eyes. Something she felt compelled to explore. "Lead on, O'Malley," she said and swung toward the house.

Chapter Eleven

Will pushed open the French doors that led from the dining room onto the rear veranda, urging Becky to walk out ahead of him. "This is my favorite view from the house."

Brushing the snow from the railing, she rested her gloved hands on it and gazed at the panoramic view of the mountains. The ranch lay in a valley running parallel to Spruce Lake. The mountains surrounding it weren't carved with ski runs, so the pines, spruce and fir marched in an unbroken mass of dark green all the way up to the tree line. Above that, the snowcapped peaks soared into a clear blue sky. "It's absolutely breathtaking," she said.

"You should see it during summer and fall. The mountains are reflected in the lake and when the sun sets behind them, it's so beautiful you'd swear you were in heaven."

"I think I'm in heaven already," Becky murmured, recognizing how much—and how quickly—she'd come to appreciate this special corner of Colorado. Yes, the town was filled with eccentric folk—and pigs—but it was also filled with kind ones. People here seemed more contented away from the stress and bustle of the city.

Her breath caught when Will stepped up behind her. His warm body pressed against her back and his big hands closed around her upper arms, melting her resolve to keep away from temptation.

"Oh…" she murmured as his lips brushed the side of her throat. Ever since their first encounter, she'd dreamed of him holding her like this, showering her with kisses. Making love to her…

Maybe it was time to see how those interrupted dreams ended….

When he turned her in his arms, she went willingly, her eyes riveted on the dark hair that sprang from the top of his shirt. He placed a finger beneath her chin, lifting it, forcing her to look into his eyes. Becky recognized in their depths a yearning to match her own. It scared her to the marrow of her bones. "W-Will?"

"Shh," he said and stroked her cheeks.

His hands trembled, confusing her. This man who could have any woman he wanted was afraid? He touched his lips to hers and Becky closed her eyes, allowing herself to feel the tenderness emanating from him. She rested her hands on his shoulders, loving the strength she felt there, craving the human contact. The warmth of his body, his hands, his mouth.

WITH A GROAN, Will wrapped his arms around Becky, needing to feel every part of her pressed against him, assuring him she wanted this as much as he did. When her fingers plunged into his hair, holding him fast as she returned his kiss, he had his answer.

For the longest time, he kissed her, tasted her, let her set the pace. If there was one thing he was sure of, it was that his judge liked to be in control.

When her mouth opened beneath his, he deepened their kiss. She met his passion with her own, sending high-voltage jolts pulsing through him. When he dared to cup her breast, she rewarded him with a moan of pleasure. He brushed the pad of his thumb over her nipple and she whimpered.

Will could feel his self-control unraveling. He should put a stop to this right now. But first, he had to taste her sweet mouth for just a little longer.

PLEASURE SURGED through Becky. She loved the sensation of his body pressed so intimately against hers, the awareness of his arousal, his warm hand cupping her breast, stroking her through the fabric of her sweater. Every nerve throbbed with excitement as she realized: *This is what I want. This is what I need.*

A woman's laughter broke through her sensual haze.

Stunned back to reality, Becky pulled her mouth from his and glanced around, certain they'd been seen.

"Relax," he murmured. "Everyone's around the other side of the house. Sound carries in the clear air."

He bent to kiss her again, but the erotic spell was broken. What was she thinking? What if someone had seen them? Becky placed her hands on his chest and pushed him away.

"Becky?"

She shook her head. "I…I'm sorry, I shouldn't have let things go so far."

She saw confusion in his eyes.

Unable to bear it, she turned away.

"Tell me what I was feeling wasn't completely one-sided," he whispered.

"It wasn't," she said, needing to be honest. "But it's been a long time for me, and I…I got carried away." She turned back to him, her face burning with embarrassment. "I'm sorry. It won't happen again." To halt any further discussion, she wrapped her arms around her and said, "It's getting cold out here. Can we continue the tour of the house?"

His reluctant nod made Becky feel like a fool. She'd hurt him. Will O'Malley might kid around, but beneath his smile beat a heart she sensed could be easily bruised. She knew all about being hurt, and she certainly didn't wish it on him. From now on, she vowed to maintain some semblance of dignity in his presence—even if she yearned to be kissed by him again.

A relationship between them wouldn't work. They were too different. Will was too carefree, while her responsibilities weighed her down. He didn't take life seriously enough. And despite the effect he was having on her, Becky was painfully aware that she was the town judge. She *had* to maintain her decorum—no matter how desperately she longed to feel like a desirable woman again.

"AND THIS IS MY ROOM," he said, opening a door and standing back to let Becky in ahead of him. They'd toured the rest of the house festooned with Christmas decorations—some made by Will's nieces.

"It's pink," she said.

"Yes, I'm so glad Sash decided to keep my decorating scheme when she moved in," he said dryly.

She laughed. "So where do you live?"

"I've moved into an apartment above Mrs. C.'s shop. Makes it easier to get to work."

"You have a job?"

"Several. Unfortunately, none of them pay." He sat on the bed, leaned back on his elbows and rested his ankle on his thigh.

That action accentuated his masculinity. Maybe a tour of the house—particularly one that included the bedrooms—*wasn't* such a wise idea. "Exactly how many unpaid jobs do you have?" she asked to cover her discomfort.

"I help Mrs. C. at her florist shop and walk Miss Patterson's dogs. Although if you'd agree to take Dugald I could devote more time to my other unpaid job—saving the buildings."

"The mayor said you threatened him and that you're gunning for his job."

Will snorted with disgust. "I said it in the heat of the moment. But he definitely needs to lose his job during the next election. If not before."

Becky crossed her arms. "So you don't have designs on city hall?"

"Not really. It's a disgrace there was no opportunity for public comment on the future of the buildings. The development plans received a speedy approval. It stinks. And so does the mayor."

Becky said nothing. Although she agreed with Will, as a judge she had to remain impartial.

"There's also your community service at the Twilight Years," she said, bringing him back to the topic—his lack of paid employment.

"Finished as of Friday."

"That was *fifty hours*. You can't possibly have completed it so soon."

"Well, I did."

He was back to being much too cocky and it grated on her. "Have you negotiated some kind of deal with the director of the home?"

"Deal?"

"To say you've done the work when you haven't." Becky could feel her irritation growing and was powerless to stop it.

He sat forward, placing both feet on the floor. "The only *deal* I have with the director of the Twilight Years was for them to adopt Edward—and for the residents to come to this fundraiser." He paused as though he'd planned to say something more, then pushed himself off the bed and headed toward the door. He was about to go through but turned back. "What is it with you? Why are you so ready to believe the worst of me?"

The anger in his tone had Becky taking a step backward. "I…I—"

"Ah, drop it!" he said, waving his hand dismissively. "I thought you were someone special, but in reality, I'm wasting my time."

He stalked out the door, leaving Becky reeling in his wake. She wasn't worth his *time?* "Just a minute!" she called and raced down the stairs to demand he apologize. But Will's legs were a lot longer than hers and he was pulling open the front door before she caught up with him.

Between the bedroom and the front hall, Becky had realized she was the one who should be apologizing. He was right; she *had* been too quick to think the worst of him. "Will!" she cried. "Please wait."

He halted, but didn't look back at her. "Wait for what? Another of your unilateral votes of nonconfidence?"

"I'm sorry. I was way out of line."

"You got that right." He released the doorknob and turned to her. "You know, Judge. What I don't get is why I don't have a problem with anyone in this town, apart from the mayor. And you. The mayor I can understand, but I have no idea why you dislike me so much."

Becky bowed her head, inhaled a deep breath and looked up at him. "I…I don't dislike you. I…have a lot of trouble trusting people."

"You seem to trust Matt just fine. Mrs. C., everyone who works at the courthouse—"

"You remind me of my father and my ex-husband," she blurted.

Will blinked. "Excuse me?"

When she didn't answer, he said, "That's reason enough to hate me, to distrust me?"

"It's complicated."

Will folded his arms. "Try me."

"It's too long a story."

"The synopsis will do."

Becky swallowed. There was no backing out of this. She'd hurt Will and needed to make amends. "If I tell you something, can I have your promise to keep it strictly between us?"

He nodded solemnly, and the intensity in his gaze convinced her she could trust him with her awful past. "My father was a gambler and a drunk. His easygoing attitude to life, the way he ran up debts, got us driven out of one town to the next."

She could feel her face burning with shame at the bald admission. The only other person in the world who knew the embarrassing circumstances of her childhood was Ben Solomon. She'd never even admitted the full truth to Graham.

Will frowned. "Sorry, don't see the connection. I don't gamble. I don't drink much. And I have no debts."

"You have no assets, either."

Will's eyes narrowed. "What would you know about that?"

"I..." Becky was starting to see the absurdity of her assumption about Will being like her father. "You don't have a job."

"Aah..." He drew the word out. "So, because I don't have a *paying* job, I can't possibly have any assets? And if someone doesn't have any assets, then he's automatically catalogued as unworthy? Wow, for a judge, you're awfully judgmental," he said mockingly and reached for the doorknob. "If you'll excuse me, *Judge,* I have guests to entertain."

"Wait!"

"For what? More insults?"

"My husband was a charmer."

"So?"

"He...could charm the birds out of the trees. Pretty much like you."

"You've lost me."

Becky's shoulders dropped in defeat. "I told you it was complicated. And I'm making a mess of this." She paced the floor of the wide entry hall. "I'm sorry...I—I've never talked about my childhood. Or my marriage. It's not easy for me to...to reveal private things. I was trying to tell you why I have a problem with trusting people."

WILL LEANED AGAINST the door. "Tell me. I need to know," he said.

Becky took a quick breath and said, "All right, if you think you're ready for the unvarnished truth."

"I am."

"Nicolas's father—his name is Graham Marcus—didn't want anything to do with him once he found out our baby wasn't...perfect."

So Nick's father had rejected him. It explained a lot about her overprotectiveness.

"I knew something was wrong when he didn't reach the physical milestones. I voiced my concerns to Graham but he pointed out how far ahead Nicolas was in his speech and communication skills. He talked in sentences at fifteen months," she said. "He could even count the number of peas in his dinner."

Will smiled as he pictured Nick, one little finger separating his peas to count them.

"Graham felt I was looking for problems that didn't exist. *His* expectations for his son were high. Too high. He was convinced Nicolas would excel both academically *and* in all the same sports he had as a youngster." She gave a self-deprecating smile. "Even going so far as to enroll him in the same schools he'd attended."

Obviously the guy had a huge ego.

"When Nicolas turned two, I insisted on having tests done and we got the diagnosis. Nicolas has cerebral palsy...." Her face was pinched with pain and Will wanted to comfort her, but she stepped away and paced the hallway again.

"I felt as if I'd been plunged into an abyss when the doctor told us what Nicolas's life would be like—even though it's a relatively mild form of CP, he might never walk, he'd need physical therapy, he could have any number of health problems as a result of his condition."

She swiped at the tears glistening on her cheeks. "Graham said nothing. He just got up and walked out of the doctor's office."

Will wanted to punch the wall. Becky's ex hadn't deserved her or their son.

"I...was devastated at the implications for my son's future and his quality of life. At first, I thought Graham had walked out because he was so distressed, but instead he..." She paused and scrubbed at her face. "He drove off, leaving us both behind at the doctor's. When I got home he refused to look at Nicolas. He said...he said..."

She fought tears, and Will wanted to pull her into his arms and tell her it didn't matter, that Nicolas was with people who cared about him now.

"He said Nicolas *revolted* him and he wanted him put in full-time care. I couldn't believe what I was hearing. How could anyone turn off his love like that—and do it to a child who needed his love and support? We had a huge fight and he blamed me for having the tests done in the first place. As if that would've made any difference!"

What sort of heartless bastard could turn his back on their child? "Did you consider doing what he wanted?"

"Of course not! Not for a second. And when…when I adamantly refused, he said…it was my choice—either him…or the…the…cripple—" Becky's voice broke and Will took her in his arms.

He let her cry it out, all the while stroking her back until she got herself under control.

"The *choice* was a no-brainer. I packed a suitcase and left that night, with my baby and the determination that Nicolas would live the best life I could give him. I went back to my maiden name and changed Nicolas's surname, too. Graham didn't care." She shook her head. "As I said, the choice was easy—but the years that followed were…very difficult.

"I had barely any money because I'd allowed Graham to control our accounts. He got me fired from the law firm, thinking that would bring me to my knees, if not my senses. So I took a job in the DA's office to support Nicolas, and I got a smart lawyer who tracked down money Graham was hiding in overseas accounts. Eventually, in exchange for keeping my mouth shut—and therefore saving his precious career and reputation—I got a settlement I could live with.

"I needed to get out of Atlanta and away from his social circle and any reminders of him, so I applied for a job in Denver that offered on-site day care. I worked long hours and hated every moment spent away from my son, but never once regretted my decision to leave my sham of a marriage.

"The whole experience reinforced my determination to protect my son from anyone who wanted to hurt him," she said as Will helped her into her coat, then pulled on his own.

That sure explained her overprotectiveness. And put it in perspective.

She took another deep breath and let it out. "Graham betrayed me so badly I swore I'd never get involved with another man. Never leave myself open to hurt and ridicule again."

And *that* explained why she'd resisted his offers of a date, of the possibility of emotional entanglement.

"Thank you for telling me that," he finally managed to say.

"Thank *you* for being a friend to Nicolas. He needs friends."

"He's a good kid. He obviously inherited your brains and not your ex-husband's."

Becky smiled at the compliment as Will opened the door, and she moved ahead of him onto the front porch. "How do you figure that?" she asked.

"Because if you were my wife, I'd never have let you go."

Chapter Twelve

Becky stumbled, stunned by his declaration. He caught her and she could feel his strength and the warmth of his body clear through the layers of her clothing. Graham had made her feel about as wanted as yesterday's trash. Will's heartfelt statement had helped restore her sense of worth as a woman. "Thank you," she said. "Both for saying that and stopping me from falling on my face." She glanced up at him. His eyes were so dark, so intense, that she believed she could lose herself in them forever.

"Mom! There you are!" Nicolas shouted, bringing her out of her trance.

Daisy and Sasha at his side, he headed toward her.

"We've been looking all over for you!" Daisy shouted. Only she didn't need to shout as they were now standing in front of Becky and Will.

"I took Becky on a tour of the house," Will said. "She really liked my pink bedroom." He winked at Sash and she broke into giggles.

All three children were eyeing Becky as if she'd been up to no good. She turned to Will and said in a formal tone, "Thank you for the tour. Your family home is lovely and I appreciate your taking the time from your busy day to show it to me." She turned back to Nicolas. "Why were you looking for me?"

"I had a brilliant idea."

"And what's that, darling?"

"You know how I need a caregiver for the holidays?"

Will coughed.

"Yes."

"And you know how none of the people you've interviewed have anything *worthwhile* to offer me?"

Becky felt herself blush. There were some opinions she shared with Nicolas that she'd prefer he not share with others. "Ah, I didn't *quite* say that."

"Yeah, you did. But I know someone you'd approve of, and I really like."

Had Nicolas met someone suitable at the barbecue? She scanned the crowd. "And whom might that be?"

"Will." Nicolas beamed and placed his small hand in Will's. "We can do lots of stuff together. Plus he can teach me to swim *and* ski."

"Excuse me?" she said in a choked voice.

"Will, Mom!" He dragged Will forward. "He needs a job, you need someone to look after me during the holidays and after school, and we're already buddies. He's perfect."

"Ah, I'm sure Will has other job prospects," she said. Employing Will would be dangerous—to her libido and her reputation—if she allowed her attraction to him to get the upper hand.

"Actually, I don't," Will said, upsetting her equilibrium further.

"I'd need references," she told him.

"If it's character references you're after, then feel free to ask around." Will indicated all the people at the barbecue.

"He's perfect for the job, Mom," Nicolas said again. "And he can teach me to swim and ski."

The swimming and skiing angle was beginning to grate on Becky's nerves. "I haven't agreed to you doing either of those activities," she said, although she could feel she was losing the battle.

"I'll take very good care of the little guy," Will told her.

"Yeah, he will!" Daisy said, and Becky wondered if the child knew how to speak without yelling.

"Uncle Will taught us to swim and ski and now we're on the ski team at school," Sasha joined in.

Becky was fast running out of excuses. "I can't understand why a man would want to spend his days caring for a young boy," she said directly to Will.

"Fathers do it all the time."

"You're not his father," she hissed and drew him aside.

"He needs a male role model."

"And someone who vandalizes expensive equipment is a suitable one?"

Will shrugged. "Aside from that. C'mon, Your Honor, you're the one who said I need a *paying* job to make me respectable."

"I didn't mean a job working for *me.*"

"Tell you what, I'll work free for the first week. If you don't like how I do things, you can send me on my way, no hard feelings."

"Your offer is tempting. However, the answer is still no. It wouldn't be appropriate."

Will combed his fingers through his hair and asked, "Does anyone ever measure up to your high standards?"

"Excuse me?"

"You heard me and you understand me, so stop playing games. I need a job. You need someone dependable to look after Nick. Do the math."

"I..."

"Save it. I've got a barbecue to run," he said and stalked off toward the barn.

She found Nicolas glaring at her. Sasha and Daisy looked equally forbidding. "What?"

"You turned him down, didn't you?" he demanded.

"Of course I did. It wouldn't be appropriate," she repeated.

"Mom, I'm eight years old. I have an IQ of over two hundred. Trust me to make at least one judgment call about people on my own." He stalked off after Will. The girls gave her identical death glares, then followed Nicolas.

Becky stared openmouthed at three retreating backs. She

seemed to be making enemies right, left and center. Perhaps it was time for her and Nicolas to head home. Only she didn't think he'd obey her and get in the car and she didn't want to make a scene.

"Enjoyin' yourself, Judge?" Becky spun around. Frank Farquar was grinning at her. "Dunno what you said to Will, but I've never seen him so steamed up."

"It's none of your business, Mr. Farquar."

"Sure it is! This is a small community. We watch out for one another. Will's hurtin' and you're the cause."

"Mr. Far—"

"The name's Frank. Can I buy you a coffee and talk to you for a bit?"

"Mr. Farquar, I see quite enough of you and your pig in court."

"Judge, you gotta drop the attitude if you wanna have any friends around here," he said and gently steered her toward the coffee wagon. "Two lattes," he ordered without asking Becky what she'd like.

While the coffees were being prepared, he said, "Your little boy has taken quite a shine to our Will. 'Course, it's not surprisin'. Everybody calls Will the pied piper of Spruce Lake."

"As I recall, the tale of the pied piper did not have a happy ending."

Frank shrugged. "Wouldn't know 'bout that. But Will's always had a way with kids. He'd be good for your boy."

And just how did Frank Farquar know about Nicolas's plans?

"I saw him being picked on when I was passin' the school week before last," Frank was saying.

"What?"

"Calm down. The O'Malley girls came to his rescue. I think young Daisy gave the big kid a black eye and probably some bruised ribs, as well."

"Nicolas was...*fighting?*" Becky was appalled. What was going on at that school? And why hadn't the teacher reported it to her?

"Nope, your boy wasn't doing the fightin', he was the victim. Daisy got the ringleader on the ground and practically had him hog-tied. Sasha told Nicolas to run and he did. Right across the road to the rec center."

Becky was nearly choking with terror. She had no idea the bullying was physical. "Why didn't you intervene, Mr. Farquar?"

He paid for the drinks and handed one to Becky. "I did. I pulled young Daisy off the other kid before she killed him. I figured your boy'd be okay 'cause I saw Will goin' into the rec center just before the fight started. Johnny wouldn't dare go after a young'un with Will around."

"You *knew* Nicolas was my son?"

"Not until today. He was gettin' a bit frantic looking for you earlier. Then I saw you comin' out of the house with Will and pointed him in your direction. Hope I didn't interrupt anything?"

"Er, no, you didn't, Mr. Far—*Frank.*" Becky took a deep breath. "I appreciate your telling me about the bullying. I had no idea Daisy and Sasha came to Nicolas's rescue. He only said he'd made some new friends at school."

"Firm friends by the looks of it." Frank sipped at his coffee and gestured at the children heading toward the barn. "You won't find better folks than the O'Malleys anywhere. Young Will's always been the one to turn his mama's hair gray with his antics. But he has a kind heart and would do anything for anyone. With all he's been doin' to save the old buildings, you'd think there weren't enough hours in the day to accomplish it all—plus all the other things he does for folks."

"Did he put you up to this?"

"Huh?" He stared at her so blankly, Becky conceded she was being unnecessarily suspicious. Yet again. She'd have to go find Will, apologize profusely, then find Nicolas and head home. Where she felt safer. In control. Sighing, she decided to take Will up on his offer—on the probationary basis he'd suggested.

She thanked him for the coffee and hurried to the barn and the strains of country-style music. It was filled with people dancing in lines. Reaching a break in the crowd, she spotted Nicolas trying to keep up with the music, Sasha and Daisy on either side of him. They giggled whenever they got the steps wrong and bumped into one another.

"Care to try some boot scootin', Judge?"

Becky felt his breath against the back of her neck like a caress. Why was he even speaking to her after the way she'd treated him? She turned and said, "Mr. O'Malley, I owe you an apology. I have it on the highest authority that you're a decent citizen."

At his raised brows, she hurried on. "And if you can forgive my rudeness, I hope you'll come and work for me." Becky had no idea how she'd keep her hands off him if he accepted, but she needed to extend an olive branch, otherwise Nicolas might never speak to her again. And by now she knew enough about Will to admit he probably *would* be good for her son.

"If you promise to stop calling me Mr. O'Malley, I might be persuaded to reconsider. Don't forget we've shared a very heated kiss." He fanned his face.

Which was yet another reason she needed to keep their relationship formal. About to point that out, she realized how controlling she sounded. "All right, *Will,*" she said instead. "But I insist on paying you, even during your probation."

He clasped her hand and shook it. "Done," he said and led her onto the dance floor.

"I can't do this!" she protested as he pulled her into the line.

"Just follow the people in front of you."

Becky tripped but Will caught her hand and, with his help, she was soon joining in.

When the band changed to a slow number, most of the dancers retired to get refreshments. Becky expected Will to draw her into the strains of the Tennessee Waltz. But Sasha bounded up to him. "Can you teach me how to waltz, Uncle Will?"

"Sure, sweetie," he said and, with a shrug of apology to Becky, led Sasha into the middle of the dance floor. Frank Farquar was pleading with Edna Carmichael to dance with him, but she steadfastly refused, standing at the edge of the floor with her arms obstinately crossed.

Becky spotted Sarah dancing with her husband. Mac

O'Malley was every bit as handsome as his sons. His face was weather-beaten but his body looked wiry and fit. Other older couples joined them and Becky smiled at the scene.

As the song ended, Sasha released her uncle and clapped her hands with glee. Then it was Daisy's turn. Becky wondered why their father wasn't dancing with his daughters, why he stood alone on the other side of the dance floor.

Will bent to whisper something in Daisy's ear. She nodded and he handed her to her Uncle Matt and went to ask Mrs. Carmichael to dance. Her face glowed as she allowed him to lead her onto the floor. Poor Frank.

After a few bars, Will waved at Frank. Becky stepped up to the older man and said, "Will's offering you the chance to cut in."

When he hesitated, she urged, "Go on. It's bad manners for a lady to refuse."

Emboldened, he tapped Will on the back. Edna's lips pursed for a moment, then she placed her hand in Frank's and was spun away before she could change her mind.

"I think they're playing our song," Will said.

"They aren't playing anything right now," Becky murmured as the band put down their instruments. The band leader announced, "We're taking a short break, folks, but we'll leave you in Dino's and Frankie's capable hands."

"Like I said, they're playing our tune," Will told her as Dean Martin crooned his classic song, "You're Nobody Till Somebody Loves You," and urged Becky onto the dance floor.

"I…don't dance. Not this kind of dancing."

"There's nothing to it," Will said, placing his hand on her back. "Relax. Let it flow."

She did, seduced by Dean Martin's beautiful baritone voice and the desire to be held by Will once again.

He sang along with the well-remembered words, and Becky smiled.

"You dance *and* sing," she remarked, needing to make conversation because what she felt in Will's arms was so wonderful—and so frightening. As if to underline her lack of control, she moved too soon and stepped on his foot.

He ignored that and said, "Mom sent us to dance lessons. My brothers hated it, but I had a crush on our teacher, so I'm much better than them."

"Modest, too." She grinned up at him. There was something charming about his lack of guile. "And the singing? You could double for Dean Martin."

"Thank you. However, I've never smoked, so I lack that husky edge to my voice that makes Dino so irresistible." He twirled her around as the music quickened, causing her heartbeat to flutter with fear that she might trip, but Will held her fast.

Becky was finding him irresistible even without the smoky edge.

When the tune segued into "You Make Me Feel So Young," Will said, "Now *that's* a fox-trot." He indicated Matt and Miss Patterson.

Dancing with a younger man seemed to make Miss Patterson feel young. *She positively glowed.* Becky smiled and said, "I think the lyrics were written just for her."

Edna and Frank were still dancing—closer this time. Couples both old and young spun by and Becky couldn't help admiring the way these old-fashioned tunes bridged the generation gap.

As the song changed again, Matt tapped his brother on the shoulder and stepped up to take Becky's hand.

"Do you mind?" he asked.

"Of course not. I was getting tired of stepping on the toes of the best dancer in Spruce Lake."

"He told you about that?"

"Uh-huh," she said and watched as Will settled Miss Patterson in a chair and went to get her some refreshments. "Although I think he was bragging because, so far, you haven't put a foot wrong."

Matt laughed and admitted, "I hated going to dance lessons. But now that I'm older, I've realized Mom had some good ideas, after all."

"Miss Patterson looked decades younger when she was dancing with you."

He gave her one of his rare smiles. "We have a permanent arrangement for at least one dance at any gathering. Have you enjoyed yourself today?"

"Very much. Your brother turned out to be quite the organizer." She scanned the room and saw Will dancing with his mother.

"He's half in love with you. You know that, don't you?"

That effectively brought her attention back to Matt. "I'm sure you're wrong." Attraction, maybe. *Love?* Impossible.

"Oh, I'm quite sure I'm right." He moved her into a quick spin, unsettling her further.

When she'd regained her equilibrium, she said, "Then perhaps it wasn't such a good idea hiring him to look after Nicolas."

"Why not?"

"Because we'll end up spending a lot of time together."

"And the problem with that would be?"

"I need to maintain a semblance of decorum. If anyone were to think I was involved in a *relationship* with an employee of mine, I'd lose the respect of those I serve."

When the song ended, Matt ordered two beers and handed her one. "Will would never seek to undermine your position. I only told you how he felt about you so you wouldn't inadvertently break his heart."

Becky nearly choked on her beer. "Break *his* heart? I'll bet your brother's left a trail of broken hearts in his wake."

"Then you'd lose the bet. For all his faults, Will's never been a player." Matt downed the rest of his beer. "Would you excuse me? I can see that a certain niece of mine would like to dance with me again."

"Of course," she said and watched as Matt headed toward Sasha, hands outstretched, then twirled her onto the dance floor.

She was both touched and impressed by the gentlemanly manners of the O'Malley men.

"Can I buy you another?"

Startled out of her musings, she turned to find Will behind

her. The man moved as silently as a cat. She gave him her half-finished beer. "No, thank you. I seem to have drunk too much coffee and beer and eaten nothing all day."

He gulped down her beer, then said, "Let's go see what's left of the barbecue."

She glanced at Nicolas, wondering if she should leave him unsupervised.

Will guessed her thoughts. "He'll be fine with his new best friends," he said. "The girls will take him back to the house when they're done here."

Becky sent him a grimace of apology. "I need to loosen up, don't I?" She allowed Will to help her into her coat as they walked out of the barn.

"Uh-huh." With his hand on the small of her back, he directed Becky toward one of the barbecue stalls.

"I hope I'll be able to rely on you to ease some of my stress regarding Nicolas's care during the holidays."

"Easy is my middle name," he said with a grin. "I'm looking forward to getting to know the little guy. He can help me with some campaigning, too, if you don't have any objection."

"As long as he's safe." She paused, considering whether she should suggest something that was important to her. "And it wouldn't hurt if you could offer him some intellectual stimulation. I don't want him falling behind just because it's the holidays."

"You really don't give up, do you?" he said, exchanging some tickets for a couple of brisket sandwiches. "The reason they have *holidays* is so their brains can recuperate from all that learning." When Becky was about to object, he held up his hand. "Don't worry, boss. In addition to being the best dancer in Spruce Lake, I also possess—thanks to all my world travel—a superior knowledge of geography. Would some *intellectual stimulation* along those lines suit you?"

Becky grinned up at him, choosing to ignore his good-natured boasting. "That would be quite acceptable."

"Plus, I'll teach him to ski."

"I haven't agreed to that."

"And swim like a fish."

Becky bit into the sandwich and sighed with pleasure. She chewed and swallowed.

"Nicolas has high expectations of himself. The girls mentioned school swim meets and other competitive things. If he fails at them, I'm concerned it'll damage his self-esteem."

"Point taken. However, I have no intention of pushing Nick to compete. This is about learning skills that will benefit him for the rest of his life. I think the fact that Nick's so smart more than makes up for any physical limitations he has on the playing field."

THAT NIGHT, LYING in bed, Becky replayed the day's events in her mind. It was long past midnight but, as usual, sleep eluded her.

What had she gotten herself into? She could only pray Will's resolve was greater than hers, because all she wanted was to feel his arms around her again, his body pressed against hers. And more than anything, his heart-melting kisses.

Chapter Thirteen

"Will!" Nicolas exited the elementary school building with a shout of welcome that told Will how much the little guy was looking forward to seeing him.

"Hey, Nick! How're you doin', buddy?"

"I'm fine, now that you're here!"

Will ruffled his red hair and wondered why he hadn't figured Nick was Becky's son earlier. He put it down to subtle differences—Becky's hair was dark red and curly, while Nick's was light red and straight. Becky's eyes were green; Nick's were blue. Becky had tiny freckles sprinkled across her nose, while Nick's face was completely covered in great big happy orange splotches that pretty much matched his hair color.

Coupled with his leg braces, that could make him a target for bullies. Frank had told him about the incident on the school grounds the day Will had first met Nick. He hadn't realized it was so bad.

A couple of the bigger boys came by. "Nicolas Ridiculous!" they sang, and Nick leaned into Will as if seeking protection. When they noticed Will, they fell silent.

"Hey. What did you call my buddy?" he asked their leader, a solid kid with a crew cut and no neck.

The kid avoided looking Will in the eye. He shuffled his feet. "Ah, nothin'. I was talkin' to someone else."

Will glanced around. "Someone else around here called Nicolas?"

The kid's lips thinned. Obviously he didn't care for being challenged by someone bigger than he was.

"You got some problem with my buddy here?" Will pressed.

"Nah."

"Good. Because I wouldn't like to hear he's being bullied. Only cowards pick on little kids. Don't they?"

The boy shrugged, looking for an escape. Another big kid came by and he slid behind him, raced down the front path and out the gate.

Will studied Nick's pinched face, worried about the effect all the bullying was having on him. "Who's that?" he asked.

"Johnny Cooper," Nick murmured, not meeting his eyes.

Will put one hand on his shoulder and gave it a squeeze. "How often does he do that?"

"Nearly every day."

"Maybe he won't now he knows you've got a buddy bigger than him."

"Really?" Nick's face shone with relief, and Will felt the release of tension in his shoulders.

To take Nick's mind off the other kid, he said, "Let's hit the pool and then we'll go over to Rusty's Grill for a burger, okay? I'll give Luke a call and see if the girls can join us." He held up his hand for a high five and Nicolas slapped it with his.

"Yeah!" Nick cried, his boyish enthusiasm returning.

The kid was endearing. How could anyone pick on someone like him? It just wasn't right.

Will took Nick's small hand and squeezed it for reassurance as they headed across the road to the rec center. "Your mom's asked me to take over morning duties with you, too, since she's so busy with all the tourists on DUI charges."

"Wow! That's so cool!" Nicolas was almost jumping out of his skin with excitement.

Will couldn't help smiling.

RUSTY'S WAS FESTOONED with Christmas decorations, complete with a miniature mountain railway scene the children admired as they ate their burgers. As Will observed the three of them, he wondered again why Becky would isolate Nick by moving him up several grades. Surely it was more important to have friends your own age than to be *challenged* all the time? And bullied…

After dropping the girls back at the ranch, they went home to Becky's.

"You two look as though you're plotting something."

Becky's voice caught them by surprise. They were sitting on the sofa, engrossed in one of Will's ski magazines, and hadn't noticed her arriving home.

"Will said he can teach me to ski like these guys, Mom!"

Becky chewed on her lip. "Will he be safe?"

"We'll stay on the children's learner slopes where they're protected from other skiers. And he'll have a helmet."

Knowing she had to learn to trust someone else with her son, she said, "All right. But *please* be careful."

"Yay! I'm gonna learn to ski!" Nicolas cried and jumped off the sofa. Both Becky and Will automatically reached out to steady him in case he fell.

Will said, "I'd better be going. I'll see you both at seven sharp." From tomorrow on, he'd get there in time to prepare Nick's breakfast and take him to school.

"Can you stay for dinner, Will? I want to show you my computer games and stuff," Nick begged.

"He might have made other plans, honey."

"I'd love to, champ," Will said and turned to Becky. "What have you got in mind?"

She looked up from unpacking her briefcase. "What I had in mind was takeout. I've been so busy at work, I haven't had a chance to shop for groceries."

Will took a good long look at Becky and saw the dark smudges beneath her eyes. He experienced a twinge of conscience for not having considered how little time she must have to herself. The town was brimming with tourists and the court would be busy.

He'd been critical of her for not spending more time with Nick. But she was juggling a career and being a single mother, which couldn't be easy, especially in a new town with no backup support. That was partly the judge's fault because she tended to cut herself off from the community, but with his help, things would be easier on her and Nick from now on. Will sure intended to make his hours with Nicolas count for something. "Then come to the ranch with me," he said. "Mom loves a crowd."

"We couldn't possibly."

"Yes, we can, Mom," Nicolas cried. "Please, please, *please* can we go? Grandma Sarah asked us to dinner when we were there today." He looked from his mother to Will. "Will Matt be there, too?"

Will smiled. The little guy had really taken a shine to his big brother. "Uh-huh. And Jack."

"Cool!" Nicolas headed for the stairs. "I'm gonna get changed."

"He's been to the ranch today?"

"The girls joined us at Rusty's for burgers after his pool session. I dropped them at home," he explained.

"If you're sure it's okay with your folks?"

Will called his mom, telling her he was bringing two more for dinner.

"She wants to speak to you," he said, holding out the phone.

FIVE MINUTES LATER, Becky hung up. Dressed warmly, Nicolas was waiting impatiently at the front door.

"Your mother is an extremely persuasive woman," she told him. "I said yes, but I'd like to bring her something."

"We can stop by Mrs. C.'s and get some flowers if you want."

Becky smiled. "That's a lovely idea. But won't she have closed by now?"

"Not for me. I live there." He opened the door and Nicolas hobbled along the front path in his awkward gait, eager to get to the ranch.

She placed her hand on Will's. "Thank you for everything you've done for Nicolas. He's...a different child with you around."

She noticed that he seemed lost for words—an uncharacteristic reaction, at least in her experience. "My pleasure," he murmured.

As it turned out, they didn't stop at the florist's. Will spotted Frank's Caddy parked in the lane beside the shop and suggested they come back another time.

On the way to Two Elk, he filled Becky in on Frank and Edna's love story. She was enchanted by his genuine caring for the older couple and his hope that they'd rekindle their love for each other.

Dinner at the ranch was a noisy affair. Nicolas and the girls were excited about being together again and kept up an incessant chatter. The rest of the O'Malleys didn't seem at all fazed by the noise as dishes were passed around the table and everyone carried on conversations. Sarah was obviously in her element, surrounded by grandchildren and by four of her five sons, eagerly wolfing down the food she'd prepared and complimenting her on it. The scene was the archetypal American family—the family she'd dreamed of having herself. The dream that hadn't come to pass…

That night, even though she was bone tired with exhaustion, Becky couldn't sleep. She punched the pillow again and rolled over to lie flat on her back, staring at the ceiling, but Will's face smiled down at her in all its dimpled glory.

What was it with the guy? By all rights she should be more attracted to Matt. He was stable, responsible, clean-cut, perhaps a little stuffy…

That gave her pause. Did people see *her* as stuffy? Had she, by trying to appear so respectable, left behind the girl in her? For that matter, had there ever really been a "girl" in her? For as long as Becky could remember, she'd been serious and responsible. She'd had to be, since her parents certainly weren't.

Maybe it was time to put all that behind her….

IN HIS APARTMENT ABOVE Mrs. C.'s shop, Will was also having trouble sleeping. After dinner, Matt had taken him aside and told him about Johnny Cooper.

Johnny's dad beat his mom, and the police were regularly called to the Cooper house by the neighbors.

"Johnny's a bully because his father is. The only way the kid feels he has any control over his life is by bullying others," Matt had said.

The situation was pretty much as Will had guessed. Unfortunately, the one most affected by Johnny's unsociable behavior was Nick.

He needed to build Nick's self-confidence and put an end to Johnny's bullying. But how?

Chapter Fourteen

Becky answered Will's knock at seven the next morning.

He passed her the newspaper, the pages well-thumbed as though he'd been sitting on her porch swing reading it, waiting for seven to roll around. The swing still rocked gently. She noted that her front path had already been shoveled and she admired his initiative.

"Morning, Your Honor," he said.

"Will!" On hearing his hero's voice, Nicolas came down the stairs as fast as his leg braces would allow, nearly tripping over his feet in his haste.

"I'll have to teach you how to slide down the banister, champ," Will said, ignoring the choked sound of disapproval from Becky. Moving toward the kitchen, he asked, "What's for breakfast? I'm starved."

Becky followed him, hustling Nicolas ahead of her. "I'm having a bagel. There's ham and eggs for Nicolas and probably enough for you, too," she said and glanced at her watch. She'd made her son's breakfast this morning, although Will had said he'd do it.

Will pulled out a chair at the table and indicated she should sit down. "Here, take a load off and eat Nick's breakfast." He slid the ham onto a plate, then gently lifted the poached eggs from the saucepan, drained them and placed them beside the ham.

"But this is for Nicolas," she protested as he went to get the coffeepot and poured some coffee into a mug. She added one sugar and a dash of cream, raised the mug to her lips, took a sip and almost purred.

Will opened the refrigerator. "What would you like for breakfast, buddy, since your mom's gobbling all the eggs?"

Nicolas chuckled and joined him. "I hope you've made out a shopping list," Will said from the depths of the fridge, "because we need to restock this thing."

Becky stifled a yawn. "Sorry, I forgot." She wiped her mouth on her napkin and started to rise. "I'll do it now."

Will's hand came down on her shoulder. "Sit. Eat," he commanded. "Champ, go change out of your pajamas, then get a pen and paper. You and I are having breakfast at Rusty's and then we're hitting the store before I drop you at school."

"Yahoo!" Nicolas yelled and limped out of the kitchen and up the stairs.

Becky swallowed her last mouthful of ham. "I'm not sure eating at Rusty's all the time is healthy."

Will crossed his arms and leaned against the refrigerator. "Relax. Rusty does a mean homemade granola, fresh-squeezed juice, ham or bacon, pancakes, eggs any style."

Becky sighed, but she did allow her shoulders to relax. She stood up. "I'll pay for your breakfasts," she said and got out her wallet.

Will closed his hand over hers. "Save it. Rusty owes me. He'll enjoy seeing Nick again, too."

Nicolas returned dressed, but with his hair still mussed, and handed paper and pen to Will. "Thanks, champ," he said. "Now, what do you need in the way of groceries?"

Becky went through the kitchen and toward the stairs, ticking off items on her fingers while Will jotted them down. She was still talking as he followed her up the stairs and into her bedroom. When he walked into her back, he stopped writing and looked at her expectantly.

"Uh, this is my bedroom," she said. "I need to take a shower and get dressed."

"So take the shower and I'll go check the pantry for anything you've forgotten."

She closed her bedroom door—and locked it, in case he decided to come in and ask if she wanted anything else.

Oh, yes, she sighed, *I want something else, but it can't be bought at the supermarket!* Becky left her bedroom twenty minutes later to squeals of excitement. Her heart fell to her stomach as she stepped onto the landing. Nicolas was sliding down the banister. Will stood at the bottom cheering him on.

She forced herself not to scream.

"Aren't these old Victorian places great?" he said. "I always wished we had a curving banister like this at the ranch." He held the shopping list in front of her eyes, but without her glasses Becky couldn't read it properly and waved it away, saying, "Fine. Great."

She pulled several large-denomination bills from her purse, handed them to Will, then bent to kiss Nicolas. She hugged him close and said, "You have a good time and behave yourself. I love you."

It was so hard to let go, but she trusted Will. "Take good care of him," she whispered as they walked out the door. "He's all I've got."

WHEN BECKY ARRIVED HOME after five, looking tired, Will suggested she put her feet up and rest while he and Nicolas joined Luke and his daughters tobogganing in Miner's Park. The park was well-lit and had a small hill, dedicated to sledding during the winter.

Nick was practically bouncing with anticipation as they piled into Luke's vehicle and headed off.

IT WAS AFTER SEVEN when Becky met them on the front porch, a frown creasing her brow. A frown that was quickly erased as Nick excitedly related his adventures.

"That's wonderful, honey," she said, smiling. She glanced up at Will. "I was getting worried. It's been dark for quite a while."

"Sorry, Judge. We were enjoying ourselves and lost track of the time." He covered her hand, which was icy cold. *How long has she been waiting out here?* he wondered and led her into the house, closing the door against the early-evening chill.

He ruffled Nick's hair and said, "He was having so much fun with Luke's girls, I couldn't tear him away."

She started to object, but he held up his hand. "Boss, you've gotta learn to let go a bit. You wanted someone to look after Nick. You've got me. He's safe. He'll *always* be safe with me."

Becky expelled an exasperated sigh. "I…I know in my head that what you're saying is true, but my heart is finding it hard to let go."

"The truth is, you don't like not being in complete control of every situation in your life."

Will knew he'd hit a sore point when she flinched. Not being a control freak himself, he found it hard to imagine why some people needed to maintain such a tight hold on everything around them.

Nicolas squealed from the living room. "There's a dog in here!"

Dugald raced up to Will, who reached down and scooped up the little dog. "What're you doing here, Dugald?"

"You know him?" Nick asked, his eyes wide with wonder.

"Sure. Dugald and I go way back, don't we, fella?" He passed him to Nick.

"He's yours?"

"No, he's yours," Becky said. "If you want him."

Nick's eyes were bigger than saucers. "Mine! Oh, boy!" He held the dog tightly. Dugald rewarded him by licking his face. "Eeyew!"

"He's only kissing you and saying hello," Will assured him as they went into the living room.

Nick sank onto the sofa and let Dugald lick his face some more. "He really likes me a lot, doesn't he?"

"Sure does," Will said, then turned his attention to Becky. "So instead of resting as you were told to, you've been visiting with Miss P.?" He shook an admonishing finger at her, but tempered it with a smile.

"I did rest. Then I remembered my promise to do something about Dugald." Her face softened with pleasure as she observed Nick and Dugald bonding.

Will massaged her neck, feeling her tension dissipate beneath his touch…and enjoying the fact that she didn't pull away. "Thanks," he said. "You've done a real favor for two people today. Dugald's going to be a great companion. Why don't we celebrate by buying a Christmas tree. The Boy Scouts are selling them down in the parking lot."

A HALF HOUR LATER, after they'd hastily eaten the sandwiches Becky had prepared, Nicolas was raring to go. With Dugald tucked in the crook of Will's arm, they were wandering through neat lines of Christmas trees. Customers roamed the aisles or warmed their hands on a fire blazing in a brazier. The stars shone brightly overhead and, with no cloud cover, the temperature had plummeted to well below zero.

The Boy Scout helping them pulled out three trees they'd shown interest in and leaned them against the fence side by side to compare.

Becky was alarmed the young Scouts wore only sweatshirts on this cold night. She and Nicolas were warmly dressed in several layers of clothing as well as ski jackets, fleecy neck warmers, beanies and gloves. As usual, Will wore considerably less.

She couldn't resist asking the young Scout who was assisting them, "Aren't you cold?"

He looked at her as though she was from another planet. "Nah. Why?"

"Because it's *cold.* And dark."

The Scout indicated a pile of ski jackets lying on a chair. "We've got 'em, but we won't need 'em."

Will bent to whisper in her ear. "We breed 'em tough up here in the mountains, ma'am."

The warmth of his breath against the tiny amount of skin

exposed between her hat and neck warmer sent tickles down her spine, making Becky forget for a moment what she'd been talking about.

"They're only out here for another hour," Will assured her. "Then they can go home."

"Another *hour?* Oh, my..."

"I like this one best," Nicolas declared. "Can we take it, Mom?"

Becky tore her eyes from the Boy Scout and looked at the tree. It was a very handsome tree. A very *tall* tree.

"Isn't it a little large for the house?"

Will sized it up. "Nope. We can put it beside the staircase where it winds up to the landing. There's plenty of height there."

"Yeah! Great idea!" Nicolas agreed.

Becky eyed the tree. There was no way it would fit in the back of her SUV—even with the rear seat down. "Can you deliver?" she asked the boy.

"Sure, we can bring it around when we close up here."

"Yay! Now we need decorations!" Nicolas insisted.

THEY GOT HOME, loaded down with decorations. Dugald had enjoyed his outing, sitting in the cart at the store, sniffing everything as it was chosen.

A truck containing their tree arrived, and the Scoutmaster and Will manhandled the Fraser fir into the house and set it up on a stand exactly where Will had said it would fit. Will lit the fire, instantly suffusing the room with warmth.

Becky stood back to check that it was in just the right place. She didn't want it blocking Nicolas's path, causing him to stumble and fall. "Perfect," she decreed.

"Yay!" Nicolas started tearing open the packs of decorations and lights.

She'd never seen her son so animated. They'd had a Christmas tree before but it was the ready-decorated, plastic, store-bought variety and definitely lacked the soul of a real tree, she decided, as the scent of fir drifted through the house.

She put on a CD of Christmas songs and soon the strains of

Neil Diamond accompanied by Will and Nicolas singing "Winter Wonderland" filled the air.

Will hung the lights on the tree, then they decorated it, Nicolas the lowest branches, Becky the middle ones and Will the topmost.

Will had a beautiful singing voice and she told him so.

He winked down at her from where he was perched on a stepladder. "Thanks, *boss,*" he said, sending Nicolas into fits of laughter.

Becky put her hands on her hips. "What's so funny, young man?"

"Will's calling you 'boss'—but I guess you are his boss." He dissolved into laughter again.

Becky's heart soared at the sound. She'd always assumed Nicolas to be a serious, withdrawn child, much like herself. But in Will's presence, he was happy and effervescent.

In another hour, all the decorations were on the tree, except one.

"Come here, champ," Will said from halfway up the stairs.

Will handed him the angel and lifted him so he could place her on top of the tree.

Becky was about to say *careful,* but managed to stop herself in time to admire Will's biceps straining against his denim shirt as he held Nicolas over the banister railing.

"There!" he said and peered down at her for approval.

"Beautiful! Let's turn on the tree lights."

Nicolas climbed onto the banister and slid down while Becky held her breath. "Wheee!" he cried and Will followed him down.

"Hold on, champ. We need to dim the house lights."

Finally, with the room lit only by firelight, Nicolas plugged the lights into the socket.

"Oh!" Becky exclaimed. It looked so much more beautiful than she'd expected. In her whole life, she'd rarely experienced such a wondrous moment as lighting this tree.

There'd been no Christmas trees during her childhood, since there was never any money to spend on that kind of indulgence. Instead, she'd snap a branch off a larger tree and bring it home to decorate with anything she could find that was shiny or pretty. But there'd been so few of those things, too. One year she'd used some of her mother's beads and been harshly reprimanded for it.

Tears filled her eyes at the memory. She'd only wanted to cheer up the trailer a little. And yet she'd been so soundly rebuked by her mother that the effect was ruined.

Becky's need to keep the details of her upbringing a secret had ensured she never got close to anyone, either professionally or in her private life. She had colleagues rather than friends and, until lately, that hadn't bothered her.

But Nicolas's exposure to Sasha and Daisy's large, close family and their very-involved grandparents had made him question why his grandparents and his father weren't part of his life. The truth—that none of them wanted anything to do with him—was too horrible to admit, even to herself. Graham's parents hadn't acknowledged any of Nicolas's birthdays or Christmases since his diagnosis, no doubt taking their cues from Graham.

To protect both her and her son from hurt, she'd cut herself off from everyone who should matter to Nicolas. Yet the O'Malleys had managed to worm their way into her heart, forcing her to confront issues so long buried she hadn't thought of them in years.

"Mom?" Nicolas's query brought her back to the present. "Why are you crying?"

She sniffed and dabbed at her eyes with the backs of her hands and tried to smile. "I'm just happy. The tree's pretty, isn't it?"

Nicolas looked back at the tree, and Becky glanced at Will. His frown told her he suspected her tears weren't only about the tree in her living room.

"Let's have some eggnog, to celebrate," she said and, without waiting for an answer, strode toward the kitchen, needing to escape Will's assessing gaze.

NICK FOLLOWED, leaving Will to ponder her tears. They'd been more than the tears of joy she claimed. Those were big, fat tears of sorrow coursing down her cheeks.

He studied the tree to see if it would reveal her secrets. It looked like every other Christmas tree that had graced his childhood home, brimming with color and light and the promise of Christmas. It said *Joy. Family. Home. Love.*

He could see Becky in the kitchen, blowing her nose. Yup, they definitely weren't tears of happiness. Something in her past had put them there. Something about Christmas…

Chapter Fifteen

The next evening, Will and Nick set off on a shopping trip. Becky was banned from it, since they were choosing her gift.

Two hours later, Nicolas bounded in the door, full of energy. "Will told off the bullies, Mom! They even shook my hand and said sorry."

"What?"

Will perched on the sofa. "We ran into them at the store and had a little heart-to-heart. I don't think Nick will have any more trouble from them."

Becky wanted to weep with joy at the incredibly wonderful feeling of having a man around to stand up for her son and "tell off" bullies. The issue had been tearing at her guts since she'd heard Johnny Cooper was still terrorizing Nicolas.

She hadn't spoken to Nicolas about why he was keeping secrets from her and mentally added that to her *to do* list.

"I'm on vacation tomorrow!" he cried, breaking into her thoughts. "Can we have pizza?"

Becky loved seeing his excitement. "Sure, sweetie."

"Cool!" he said and dashed into the kitchen.

Becky noticed he was more stable on his feet and moved more fluidly. She smiled up at Will. "Thank you for doing that. I couldn't get an appointment to see his teacher until after the holidays."

"Nick told me." Lowering his voice, he said, "Between you

and me, I don't think this is over, but Nick's going into the holidays feeling happy. I still don't trust that Cooper kid an inch, but you should've seen the look on Nick's face when Johnny shook his hand. He was so relieved."

"But what about January, when he's back at school? He might come after him again."

Will placed a calming hand on her shoulder. "I'll talk to Nick and help him with some strategies for dealing with bullies. But for now, I want him to relax and enjoy himself. I'll be with him all the time, so he'll be safe."

Becky released her breath. Will was right; Nicolas should be allowed to enjoy his holidays without any fears. "Thank you for everything. You've exceeded my expectations of a caregiver in every possible way."

"You're welcome. It's all part of the service."

Becky knew it was much more than just "part of the service." "I've set aside time to come to the pool tomorrow to watch him swim," she said.

Will rewarded her with a grin so wide, her heart turned over.

NICOLAS KEPT GLANCING at her to make sure she was watching as he did his therapy. Becky waved back enthusiastically and gave him a thumbs-up.

"Hi, boss," Will said as he joined her, rubbing a towel through his wet hair. "The little guy sure loves the pool, doesn't he?" He stretched out his long legs as he sat on the bench.

Becky concentrated on keeping her eyes trained on her son and not on Will's half-naked body.

Nicolas became even more animated once Will arrived. He began to show off a little and she couldn't help smiling at his obvious hero worship. Her son was thriving—and Will was responsible.

"Catch you later. I do my laps while the little guy does his therapy," Will said and strode through to the pool.

Becky watched him leave, her throat dry.

AFTER NICOLAS'S THERAPY session, it was time for his swimming lesson with Will. Tears sprang to Becky's eyes. Her precious son could swim! Okay, he wasn't going to be winning races anytime soon, but he had the basics. His breathing was good, his arms thrashed the water and propelled him along, while his legs trailed behind. He looked so proud of himself as Will towed him back to the pool's edge.

"I'm really impressed with you, sweetie," she said as Will lifted him out of the water to sit on the pool's edge. "You're doing *great.*"

"Really, Mom?" His eyes shone with happiness.

She knelt down to hug his wet body, uncaring of what the chlorine might do to her clothes. "You're a much better swimmer than me already." She wrapped his towel around him.

"Wow! Did you hear that, Will? Maybe you can teach Mom to swim so she can keep up with me."

Will hauled himself out of the pool in one easy movement to stand in front of her, his hair dripping wet. Lord, he was magnificent. All rippling muscles and sinewy strength. She'd have to get through her cases faster so she could make it to the pool more often.

Will grinned and Becky's legs nearly gave out under her. "Sure," he said, looking into her eyes. "I'm happy to teach your mom anything she wants."

Heat suffused her face. It sounded as if Will intended to teach her something altogether different from swimming....

THAT EVENING, NURSING a glass of wine as she rested on the sofa while Will and Nicolas cleaned up after dinner, Becky knew she'd made the right decision in employing Will. The difference in Nicolas was astounding. He seemed stronger every day, his appetite had improved and his complexion glowed with health. Instead of being shut up in her chambers after Jessie dropped him off following hydrotherapy, he now went with Will on a circuit of the town, Dugald in tow.

I could get used to this, she thought and smiled at Dugald having doggy dreams on his bed in front of the fire, his tiny legs making running motions in the air.

She could get very used to getting home to delicious aromas from the kitchen and the sound of her son horsing around with Will.

Although she'd come here reluctantly, she was beginning to feel a part of this community and regretted her initial attitude, which had clouded her opinion of Spruce Lake.

Many of the problems—drunk driving, drugs, traffic violations and so on—were perpetrated by outsiders, hence the reason court was so busy this time of year. Thankfully, the town's number-one public nuisance, Louella Farquar, and her outrageous antics, were nearly a distant memory.

And the way the community had rallied behind the cause of saving the old buildings was impressive.

An ideal town to raise a family. Now where had that come from? Probably Sarah O'Malley when she'd dropped by to take her to lunch that week.

Will's mom had done a sales job on the town, and on her son, adding snippets praising the town as a safe place to live and raise a family....

"Hey, Mom!" Nicolas jolted Becky from her musings as he jumped onto her lap. Her wineglass tilted alarmingly but a large hand swooped in to wrap around hers and Will removed the glass from danger.

"Thanks." Becky glanced up at him and smiled. Since taking over Nicolas's care, he hadn't made a single pass at her. Granted, she'd warned him to be on his best behavior, but since when did Will do as he was told? She'd half expected to be beating him off with a stick, yet he'd been the embodiment of professionalism and a gentleman to boot.

Will ruffled Nicolas's hair and Becky's heart warmed. He felt genuine affection for her son and wasn't afraid to show it. They made an easy trio, lounging on her comfy old sofa with the fire blazing in the grate. *Like a family.*

She worked at quashing that thought as soon as it entered her head.

"Will and I are going out for ice cream. Wanna come?"

She pulled a fleecy blanket over her legs. "No, sweetie, I'm enjoying myself right here. Why don't you guys bring me some back?"

"Go put on some more layers before we head out, champ."

"But you don't wear big heavy jackets," Nicolas protested.

"That's 'cause I grew up here and I'm a tough mountain man," Will told him in a deep voice that had Nicolas chuckling.

Becky shook her head. "You really will catch your death of cold one of these days," she warned as Nicolas went to collect his gloves, hat and jacket.

Will leaned close. "Not while I have you to keep me warm," he murmured, but Becky was the one who felt her face heat.

Chapter Sixteen

"Get up, Mom! Will's got a surprise for us!" Nicolas jumped on her bed, followed by Dugald.

This was Saturday, so she'd been hoping to sleep in, but lately Nicolas was so full of energy, he was often up before her.

"I don't think I could possibly eat another meal at Rusty's," she muttered.

"How does breakfast in bed sound?" Will was standing in her bedroom doorway, a tray in his hands.

"It sounds—and smells—wonderful," she said. "But you don't have to work weekends."

Will set the tray on the bed beside her. "I'm not working, but I thought you might both enjoy a surprise." He placed a bowl containing dry dog kibble on the floor for Dugald. With a bark of excitement he leaped off the bed and stuck his nose in his food.

Becky surveyed the tray. A mug of coffee for her and one of hot chocolate for Nicolas. Bagels, cream cheese, ham, two poached eggs, two bowls of diced fruit. "There's only breakfast for two here."

"Yup. Enjoy yourselves. I'm heading out to the ranch, then I'll be back for the surprise."

"I thought this was it."

Will grinned. "Nope. Dress warmly and I'll see you in forty-five minutes." He whistled as he left the room.

"What do you suppose that's about?" she asked.

Nicolas shrugged. "Beats me. He wouldn't even tell *me* where we're going. But knowing Will, it's gonna be something really special."

"Going to," she corrected, bit into a piece of apple and wondered what this intriguing man was up to now.

"WHERE'S YOUR VEHICLE?" she asked as Will opened the passenger door of a battered old truck. Bales of hay were stacked in the truck bed. Nicolas scooted across and sat in the middle of the bench seat. Will put Dugald on his lap, then offered his hand to assist Becky into the truck.

"I don't bite," he said when she hesitated.

She settled onto the seat. "I just didn't expect you to help me."

"Get used to it, darlin'," he said and closed the door firmly.

THE COUNTRYSIDE they drove through was breathtaking. Overnight snow carpeted the landscape, and it was so pristine, so achingly beautiful, Becky sighed with pleasure.

"It does that to me, too, sometimes," Will said from across the cab. "I think you'll enjoy our destination."

Twenty minutes later, they turned into a narrow valley and continued along it for several miles. The valley widened as they drove farther and as the panorama opened up, the effect was as if someone had unwrapped a beautiful gift. Snowcapped mountains rose on either side of the valley. A river, partly iced over, burbled beside the road. Sunlight bathed the valley floor, and the snow glistened like billions of tiny diamonds spread across the land.

"I've never seen anywhere so beautiful," Becky breathed in wonder.

Will grinned at her as he turned off the road, then lowered the plow on the truck's front end. The vehicle easily pushed the fluffy powder snow aside as they drove into an open field.

Becky spotted a large, brown mass in the distance. "What's that?" she asked, squinting. Dugald's ears pricked up and he put his paws on the dashboard to steady himself while he sniffed at the air.

"It's elk, Mom!" Nicolas shouted. "Oh, boy, oh, boy, oh, boy!"

Realization dawned on her. "And the hay is for the elk?"

"Uh-huh."

Will climbed out and helped Nicolas down from the truck. Dugald leaped out and raced toward the elk, but the snow was so deep he disappeared in a white clump. All they could hear was muffled barking as the clump moved of its own accord.

Becky laughed so hard at the antics of her pint-size dog she had tears running down her face.

"Oh, dear, that's about the funniest thing I've ever seen!" she cried, while Nicolas dug Dugald out.

The little dog shook off the snow and started barking to warn the humans of imminent danger.

"Hey there, buddy." Will scooped him up and placed him in the truck bed. "You can guard the pickup, but you've gotta keep quiet, okay? Those elk aren't going to hurt us." He petted the dog and talked to him in soothing tones and soon Dugald relaxed and jumped atop one of the hay bales, keeping his eyes on the elk. Will hauled off the rest of the bales and threw them on the ground several yards from the truck. The elk lifted their noses to the wind, looking interested. Once all the bales—except Dugald's—were arranged on the snow, he clipped the wire surrounding them to release the hay.

Several elk wandered toward them but halted when Dugald began to bark again.

"Dugald! Hush!" Will commanded and the dog sat in silence as the elk edged closer.

Becky held her hand to her mouth to quell her emotions at the sight of these wild animals walking toward them, sniffing at the hay, then tearing chunks off the bales. "I've never seen anything like this in my life. What a perfect surprise," she said, placing her hand in the crook of Will's arm. "Thank you for bringing us here."

He covered her hand and squeezed it. "You're welcome."

"Why are you feeding them?"

"Elk lose around thirty percent of their body weight during normal winters. If it's particularly harsh or long, then their survival is severely compromised. We're expecting a big storm tonight and a lot of snow for the next few weeks. I like to give them a helping hand."

Becky's admiration for him took another leap forward. Will was not only a wonderful friend to her son, he was a complete humanitarian.

"Who owns the land?" she asked, unable to take her eyes off the animals.

"I do."

She glanced up at him and stepped away. "And now you're pulling my leg."

Will dug his hands into his pockets and grinned down at her. "No, I'm serious. I bought it over ten years ago with my first paycheck from the movies."

"You really like turning my preconceived notions about you upside down, don't you?"

"I'm not doing it on purpose. Your misconceptions are based solely on the fact that I appeared in your court."

"You're absolutely right and I apologize for not only pre-judging you but also *mis*judging you."

"Apology accepted. Now, will you agree to come out on a date with me?"

"You don't give up, do you?"

"Nope. Not when I want something this badly."

"But you're my employee."

"So marry me and I'll look after Nick for free."

She laughed at his outrageous suggestion. "Don't tempt me."

Will reached out and pulled her closer. "Seriously?"

She batted his chest. "No, of course I'm not serious!"

"Mom! Look! The elk are coming to me," Nicolas interrupted just as things could've gotten interesting. "What'll I do, Will?"

"Stand your ground, buddy. You can grab a bunch of hay and feed them if they'll take it from you."

"Is it safe?" Becky asked, unable to ignore her motherly concerns. "They *are* wild animals."

"Wild, but friendly. Look."

A calf approached and tugged gently at the hay Nicolas proffered. "I wish I had a camera," she said in wonder.

Will produced a small digital camera. "Snap away."

She spent the next few minutes taking shots of Nicolas with the baby elk. Then Will took photos of her and Nicolas with the calf. Then Nicolas took photos of Becky, Will and the elk. Becky finished the photo shoot, concentrating on the valley scenery. "I want to remember this forever and I'd love to get some of these enlarged," she said, handing the camera back to Will.

"Good idea." He produced a thermos of hot chocolate and a box of cookies. "Care for a picnic among the elk?"

"Yeah!" Nicolas grabbed a cookie.

Touched by Will's thoughtfulness, she helped take lawn chairs from the truck's tray and set them up so they could watch the elk feeding, with the snowy mountains as a backdrop.

Nicolas went off to throw a ball for Dugald in the plowed area, successfully distracting the little dog from the animals grazing so close to them.

Settled in the chairs, their hands wrapped around mugs of hot chocolate, she asked, "How much land do you own?"

"Only two hundred acres."

Becky sputtered. *"Only?"* Although she was aware ranches were considerably larger than that in Colorado, two hundred acres sounded like an awful lot to her.

"What are you going to do with it?"

"I *had* planned on building a cabin and moving here. I love the serenity. And the views."

"You'd raise cattle?"

"Nope. I planned to kick back on my porch and watch the wildlife roam. I get the occasional moose down by the river. Bears are hibernating in the hills, but they come out to forage for berries during the summer. There are foxes, lynx, lots of squirrels—all sorts of critters. Why spoil it with smelly old cows?"

"True!" She looked around at the vista again, taking in the river with steam rising off it into the chilled air. Away from the cleared flat bottom of the valley, pine, spruce and aspen stretched up the hillsides. And everywhere was the all-encompassing majesty of the mountains. "Oh, Will, how lucky you are to own a piece of paradise."

"Yeah," he agreed. "But I might not own it for long."

NICOLAS THREW THE BALL to Dugald while keeping an eye on his mom and Will. Everything was working out just the way he wanted it to. It made him feel good seeing them together. He'd seen how they looked at each other....

He loved Will and would be thrilled to have him as his dad. Then Sash and Daisy would be his cousins and they could hang out together all the time. He could stay in Spruce Lake instead of going back to Denver and that school his mom kept raving about. Didn't she understand it was better to have real friends instead of competitors? His mom was happy when he'd aced the entrance exam. So what? He hadn't even tried and he'd still got top marks, so what could the school teach him? Nothing he couldn't read in books or learn online. But Will taught him new things every day, important things you couldn't learn anywhere else.

And Will's family treated him as if he was *normal*. He liked that. His mom's colleagues in Denver were so patronizing, either talking about him as if he wasn't there or he was fragile or something.

He loved fooling around with Matt and Jack, and although he'd been a bit scared of Luke at first, he'd studied some Internet sites on horse breeding and they'd had a long conversation about it over dinner the other night. Luke liked talking horses and had offered to teach him to ride since Will was allergic to horses. He couldn't wait!

He was gonna have to choose his moment to talk to his mom about staying in Spruce Lake. Maybe she could set up a law practice here or the judge she was standing in for would decide she didn't want to work now she had a little baby. Yeah, that would be perfect!

Except…his mom was frowning. That wasn't good.

"WHY WON'T YOU OWN IT for much longer?" Becky asked and tightened her ponytail.

"Turns out this spread has increased in value over the years. Jack and Matt suggested I sell it and use the funds to buy back the old buildings."

"It galls me that you'd have to give up this stunning piece of property. But realistically, do you think the development company would sell?"

He lifted a shoulder. "I'm hoping the strength of public opinion will make them rethink their plans. If they do pull out, then we need to have the funds available to step in and buy the property before another developer snaps it up. The way the town bylaws read at present, the buildings won't be safe until someone who genuinely wants to preserve them actually owns them."

"A noble idea, but the real estate they're sitting on is worth a lot of money. I can't see that leaving the old buildings as they are would be commercially viable."

He tapped the side of his nose. "Jack and I have some ideas."

"Want to share them with me?"

Will basked in her interest. "Okay. For starters, none of them have foundations. They're just sitting on the ground they were built on. Lucky for us we don't get tornadoes through here, otherwise half the town would've been over in another county long before now."

Becky laughed and he savored the sound of it. "Now that's an interesting visual!" she said.

"We plan on excavating new basements and moving the buildings onto them. They're set out in a pretty haphazard way that doesn't make the most of the site. By tidying it up and making access easier, we can build a small condo complex with a Victorian facade that complements the site. Once the old buildings are on their new foundations, we'll renovate the siding and interiors. The houses and condos would fetch good prices since they're within easy walking distance of the ski lifts. The other buildings would have shops on the first floors and apartments on the upper floors, much like Mrs. C. has over her shop. That'll bring both commercial and residential life back to that end of town."

Becky clapped her hands. "Brilliant!"

Delighted by her response, he said, "I need to get this land properly valued and find an interested buyer."

"I admire your determination to save those buildings, but it would be such a shame to give up this beautiful land."

"It isn't big enough for a viable ranch, but it's the perfect size to carve up into what they call ranchettes—around five to ten acres each."

"That's an appalling idea! All this beautiful open space covered in houses!"

Will couldn't help grinning at her heartfelt dismay. "It's not as bad as you think. There's a huge demand for people wanting homes within a ten-mile drive of the town and ski area but who also want the wide-open spaces of Colorado around them. Jack took me to see a similar development in the next county. With strict building covenants regarding the style of homes, setbacks, natural landscaping and the need to preserve as much of the natural environment as possible, it could work well."

"But what'll happen to the elk and the other animals?"

"I plan on keeping back a hundred acres for a wildlife corridor." At least that would ensure the vacant land couldn't be used for any activities that would threaten the wildlife.

"If you keep half the land, I can't see how it would be enough to buy the old buildings."

"I didn't think so, either. But according to Jack's research, each ranchette property would sell for ten times what I initially paid for all the land."

"Oh, my..."

Will had mixed feelings about selling but was thrilled the land had increased so much in value and he could put it to good use. "Exactly." He smiled. "When he said I should be able to keep a hundred acres for myself, it was pretty much a no-brainer."

"And if this all works out, what happens to the money that's already been raised?"

"Any fundraising money will be put straight back into the community, with interest. There are plenty of projects needing funds."

Impressed by the way he'd thought all this through, she said, "In that case, I can't see anyone in the town objecting to your plans—apart from the mayor."

"The mayor likes being mayor. If he gets the development company to sell to us, then he'll benefit by appearing to be a great negotiator. Not to mention that the town benefits from a worthwhile project, and you can be sure he'll be first in line to take the congratulations on that!"

She laughed. "You know him so well."

"Unfortunately, yes. And as much as it annoys me to pander to his ego, if it serves my purpose, then I'll schmooze the guy to get what I want."

"Sounds like it's time for a new mayor."

"He's been seduced by the development company. I told him if he doesn't back down, I'll run against him in the next election."

"So he told me!" Becky laughed.

"I'll do just about anything to save those buildings."

"Judging by how much the town's behind you, you'd win. And what would you do then, Mr. Mayor?"

"Order you to marry me?"

She slapped him playfully, enjoying their banter. Will was entertaining company, intelligent, determined, ambitious—when it suited him. All the things she'd assumed he wasn't, simply because he'd appeared before her on a misdemeanor. "Okay, I'll agree to one date." She held up her index finger. "But only when you're no longer my employee."

He grinned. "If I really want something, then I'll find a way to get it. And I want you that badly."

Her face suffused with heat at the insinuation in his words. To cover her discomfort, she got to her feet and said, "I think we should be getting back. Nicolas and I have Christmas shopping to do and I don't want to keep you from relaxing on your day off." Since they'd been invited to the O'Malley ranch for Christmas Day, there were more gifts to be purchased.

"Why do you do that?"

"What?"

He cocked his head and studied her. "Shut me out when I want to get close."

"Will, we both know a long-term relationship between us isn't going to work."

He stood up to tower over her. "Only because you won't give it a chance."

She sighed. "Look, I come with a lot of personal baggage attached. You, on the other hand, have had an ideal upbringing. You've got a carefree nature and—"

"You're sure about that?"

"What could you possibly have to worry about?"

"Ever wonder why Matt and I were on the kiddie slopes instead of up on the mountain skiing?"

"The thought had crossed my mind." Becky couldn't even begin to imagine where this was heading.

"Ever wonder why I quit a lucrative job in the movies?"

She folded her arms. "Yes. You're at the peak of physical fitness. You seem born to ski, live an outdoor life. Why *did* you quit?"

"Because I nearly died in an avalanche."

Becky felt the blood drain from her face. "You…you nearly…*died?*" She touched his arm, as though by touching him she could assure herself he was real. Alive. "What happened?"

"It's a long story."

"I want to hear it." She slid her hand down his arm and caught his hand in hers.

And so he told her.

WHEN HE'D FINISHED, she placed her hand against his cheek. Her voice hoarse with emotion, she said, "Thank you for sharing that with me. I know it took a lot of courage."

Will covered her hand, apparently unable to speak.

Nicolas wandered up to them, his gaze taking in their joined hands. Hers gloved, Will's bare.

"Ready to go and do that last-minute shopping, sweetie?" she asked, needing to distract him.

Will hefted the chairs into the back of the truck. "Don't feel obligated to buy presents for the family. There are way too many of us. Besides, your presence is gift enough for Mom."

"That's very kind, but I wouldn't dream of spending Christmas with your family without bringing something."

Will took down the bale Dugald had been sitting on earlier, clipped the wire and put it out for the elk. The little dog was so exhausted from running around in the snow, he was curled up on the front seat of the truck, fast asleep, as they drove away from the grazing elk.

THAT EVENING WILL STAYED for dinner. He and Nicolas prepared spaghetti Bolognese while Becky luxuriated in the bath.

Throughout dinner, Will couldn't keep his eyes off her. He'd tried so hard to maintain a professional distance, but it wasn't working. She avoided his eyes and kept up the chatter with Nick, who was bragging about having beaten him at Trivial Pursuit.

Finally, she met his eyes and said with a smile that warmed his soul, "You do realize he's memorized all the answers, don't you?"

"I realized it the first time we played, so I went and bought the latest edition. He pretty much knew those answers, too." Will pulled a mock frown and Becky laughed outright. He loved it when she forgot she was his boss or the town judge and was just Becky. A mother, proud of her son. A sexy woman…

Whoa, there! he warned himself. *Gotta keep that professional distance.*

But his plans went haywire as soon as Nick was tucked up in bed.

He'd brought a CD and left it playing during dinner and was humming along when Becky returned from saying good-night to Nick.

"Thank you for suggesting I adopt Dugald," she said, coming into the kitchen. "That little dog has made such a difference to Nicolas. And so have you. He's a different child these days," she said and kissed his cheek.

For a moment, they both stood frozen, as if equally shocked by her gesture. And then Will did the only thing he could think of to defuse the situation. He drew her to him and spun her around, dancing her into the living room.

Bad move, he decided when he saw how dimly lit the room was. And now Dean Martin was singing his favorite song! *Really bad move.*

"Sing to me," she whispered against his throat.

Will's mouth was so dry, he wasn't sure he could even hum it without faltering, but he gave it his best shot.

Becky rested her head against him, which made him miss a note. He cleared his throat and continued, concentrating on the lyrics to take his mind off what he really wanted to do with Becky.

"I could listen to you sing all night long," she sighed wistfully as the song ended.

Night. She shouldn't have said that. It conjured up all sorts of erotic images.

When he didn't respond, she stepped back. He could see, even in the lamplight, that she was blushing. "I…I'm sorry. I didn't mean it to come out that way."

"Hush," he murmured, still holding her loosely, holding her gaze, daring her to look away.

When she didn't, he traced her bottom lip with his thumb. She expelled a breath and her eyes closed.

"Look at me," he said, and when she opened her eyes, he knew she wanted this as much as he did.

He cupped her cheeks and touched his mouth to hers, tentatively at first and then deepening the kiss when her fingers increased their pressure on his arms.

He was surrounded by sensations: her taste, her scent, the tiny whimpers that escaped her, the softness of her lips and, most especially, the urgency implied by the way her fingernails dug into him, drawing him closer.

But this couldn't go any further, not with Nick upstairs.

He took her upper arms and gently pried her hands away.

"Wha—"

Confusion filled her enticing green eyes. He hated doing this to her. To him. Fighting to control his breath, he said, "I'm sorry. I got carried away."

"I didn't mind."

He touched a finger to her lips and said, "I know."

Unable to bear the hurt and confusion in her eyes, he released her and turned away, brushing his hand through his hair.

When he'd gotten his breathing under control, he looked back at her. "I'd better go. I'll see you in the morning."

"Will—"

"I'm going, because if I stay, I'll never be able to leave. You don't want that. Good night, *boss,*" he said, to reinforce to both of them that they needed to get their libidos under control, at least until he was no longer her employee.

He closed the door behind him.

STUNNED AT WILL'S SUDDEN departure, Becky stared at her front door for several minutes, forcing the tears that threatened not to fall. At first she'd thought he was rejecting her, but his parting words allayed that fear.

A tiny smile curved her mouth as she headed upstairs to bed.

Chapter Seventeen

"Is it really okay for me to stay at the ranch tonight, Mom?"

Becky and Nicolas had joined the O'Malley family in the town square to participate in the annual Carols by Candlelight event. Afterward they'd all gather at Two Elk for dinner.

Becky smiled down at her son. "Yes, sweetie, if that's what you'd like."

"Yes!" Nicolas punched the air.

"You'll need to pack your pajamas and some clothes for the morning."

"And your toothbrush," Will put in.

"Wow, my first sleepover!" he cried and high-fived Luke's daughters. Then he sobered. "Are you sure you won't be lonely without me tonight?"

Becky's heart filled with love. Nicolas was such a sweet, considerate child and she was so lucky to have him. She hugged him and said, "Of course not. I'll have Dugald for company."

Nicolas frowned, as though debating whether this was a fair exchange. During the past week he'd learned to ski—strictly on the kiddie slopes. Will claimed he was one of the fastest learners ever, earning Becky's gratitude for saying so in front of her son.

An outing to the Denver Museum of Science and Nature was also a huge hit, not least because Sasha and Daisy had tagged along. And Luke was teaching him to ride. Her son's days were filled with activity—and some intellectual pursuits sprinkled in for good measure.

Light snow began to fall as they walked back from the park. By the time they got to Becky's, it was coming down in fat, lazy flakes.

"Looks like we'll have a white Christmas," Will remarked as he held open the door and hummed a few bars from "White Christmas." He grinned. "Snow's forecast all through the week."

"Oh, boy!" Nicolas cried. "My first white Christmas in the mountains *and* my first sleepover! Life doesn't get any better than this." He tore upstairs to pack an overnight bag.

BECKY TURNED AND WATCHED the lights of the ranch fading into the distance as they drove back to town after dinner. Snow was still falling, but Will negotiated the roads with practiced ease. "Having second thoughts?" he asked.

She turned to face forward. "Not about the sleepover. I'm so happy for him, but also a little sad that this is the first night we won't be together."

He reached over and gave her knee a comforting pat. "It's a perfectly natural reaction. I loved seeing the excitement in his eyes. This is about the happiest I've seen that little guy."

She was about to cover Will's hand to impart her gratitude for all he'd done for Nicolas but he took his hand away to make a sharp turn.

"I know I keep saying this, but I really want to thank you. Nicolas is a different child in so many ways and I know a lot of that's due to you."

Will smiled across at her. "You're welcome. Spending time with him has enriched my life."

The admission surprised her. "How so?"

"The first time I met him at the pool, he was such a spunky little guy. He came right up to me and said, 'Hi,' like he was so self-assured. But I sensed a vulnerability and I…wanted to protect him." He shrugged. "I know it's natural for parents to feel protective toward their children, but something about Nick reached deep down inside me. I wanted to help him live life to the fullest. He's so courageous and he'll grab every opportunity with both hands and do the best he can."

Becky's heart swelled at Will's insight and his desire to help her son. In a moment of uncharacteristic impulsiveness, she took his hand, brought it to her mouth and kissed it. And then, unable to resist, she turned his hand over and placed her lips on his palm.

WILL NEARLY STEERED the vehicle off the road. The sensation of her moist lips touching his palm had his body responding instantly. He fought the wheel, trying to bring his SUV back in control—or at least under more control than his hormones.

"Ah, sorry about that. Slight lapse in concentration," he said and glanced across at Becky. She was grinning at him.

She knew exactly what she was doing! He grabbed her hand and laid it on his thigh. Then moved it lower, toward his knee, not wanting her to know how serious that lapse in concentration really was.

Not yet.

"YOU SAID YOU WEREN'T having second thoughts about Nick's sleepover," Will said as they pulled up outside her house. He switched off the ignition. "So, what *are* you thinking about?"

"Inviting you in for a nightcap." There it was. She'd as much said she wanted him in her bed. Because wasn't that what the question implied when it was posed in the movies? *A nightcap* was a euphemism for *sex*.

Becky couldn't believe her audaciousness, but for too many nights she'd lain awake dreaming of Will.

When he didn't say anything, she reached for the door handle, feeling like a fool, but Will caught her elbow and drew her back to face him. "Are you sure you know what's usually meant by a *nightcap?* Because it often means, 'Come inside and let's make love.' However, it can also mean, 'Come inside and have a brandy or a cup of coffee.' I want to be absolutely sure of what you're asking."

She swallowed. Cursing the quaver in her voice, she said quietly, "Which one would you say yes to?"

"Both," he told her, without hesitation.

She couldn't hide her happiness. "Really?"

"Yes. *Really.*"

Suddenly self-conscious, she turned away. "I was so afraid you'd say no."

He grasped her chin and turned her to face him again. "I've wanted to make love to you since the moment we met."

With shaking hands, she fumbled with her door handle. By the time she'd managed to open it, Will was there to help her out. Unable to meet his eyes and the intensity of his gaze, she forced strength into her legs and marched up her front path.

As soon as they were inside, Will kicked the door shut and pinned her against it, his hands cradling her face, his lips working their magic, convincing her this was *right.* His take-charge attitude, combined with tenderness, excited her. His kisses melted her. He wrapped his strong arms around her. And she loved it.

When they finally came up for air, he said, "What's next?"

Yes, what was next? Becky slipped out of his arms. She'd never seduced a man and wasn't sure of the protocol.

"Would you like coffee or a drink?" she asked to hide her nervousness and strode into the kitchen.

"Neither," he murmured, stepping up behind her, setting all her nerve endings on alert.

The light of the lamp on the table in the hallway created an intimate mood. "Now, where were we?" he asked, lifting her hair and kissing the nape of her neck, sending delicious sensations shimmying through her.

Becky sighed. She wanted this so much. Wanted *Will* so much. He made her yearn for things she couldn't have. But maybe, just for one night, she could.

He pulled her back against him, nuzzling her neck.

It felt wonderful to be held so close. So close that she was aware of Will's very male reaction.

She turned, slid her arms around his neck and said, "Make love to me, Will. Please?"

Chapter Eighteen

"Are you sure about this?"

"Absolutely!"

He smiled at her enthusiasm.

This man is too good to be true, a tiny voice kept nagging her. She recognized it as the *Voice of Experience* and pushed it away, thinking, *But he loves my son. He cares about people, about this town. About me.* They were powerful affirmations.

"I can sense you're still not positive," he said, breaking into her thoughts.

"Okay, I'm scared," she admitted, her shoulders sagging with defeat.

"Of…me?"

"Of being hurt again."

He kissed her temple and murmured, "Don't be afraid. You're safe with me. I'll always keep you safe. You…and Nick."

She stroked his cheek. "Thank you. I needed to hear that."

Will kissed her. A gentle peck to the end of her nose, a touch of his lips to her closed eyelids and then tender kisses to her mouth, exciting her, making her crave more. Ever so slowly, he drove the last of her inhibitions away. His tongue teased her mouth, then gained entry.

She gasped when he slipped his hand beneath her sweater, touching the bare skin of her back, stroking her—driving her wild with want, with need.

When he unclipped her bra and cupped her breasts, she delighted in his grateful sigh as they fell into his hands. She felt empowered, beautiful, desired. And still he continued to kiss her.

The exquisite sensation of his callused thumbs caressing her breasts made them swell beneath his touch.

Will smiled against her mouth. "You like that?" he whispered.

"You need to ask?"

With a growl of male satisfaction, he grazed her throat with his teeth.

She'd never experienced anything so sensual before. Will's lovemaking made her *want* to feel wanton, to let her defenses completely down and succumb to whatever pleasures he wished to bestow.

Desperate to touch him, she reached beneath his sweatshirt and ran her hands over his back.

"Take it off," he said against her throat.

She complied, pulling the sweatshirt over his head, then at the sight of his half-naked body in the lamplight, she pressed a kiss to his chest, savoring his male scent and the warmth of his skin.

"I LIKE THAT," HE GROANED and held her close, enjoying her feminine softness. He needed Becky and told her so as he dropped moist kisses on her throat. She rewarded him with a sigh that spoke of her need and sent his libido into overdrive.

If they kept on like this, he wouldn't make it to the bedroom.

He loved caressing her, teasing her, taking her higher with each kiss. "You feel beautiful," he murmured and pulled up her sweater, exposing her to him. He kissed her breast, too impatient with need to strip her sweater off all the way.

"Oh!" she gasped as he drew an erect nipple into his mouth, driving himself nearly crazy with need. He had to put a stop to this *now!*

With more self-control than he believed he possessed, Will pulled her sweater back down, took her hands in his and said, "We need to get a room."

"I happen to have one upstairs," she said, thrilling him with her eagerness.

"Are you sure about this?" he asked again. "I don't want any morning-after regrets."

"I've tried so hard to resist you." She sighed against his chest, unable to meet his eyes. "And I can't find one good reason to resist you anymore."

"Hallelujah!"

She grinned up at him. "Why were you so persistent?"

"I fell in love with your red hair and green eyes. And your freckles." He kissed the tip of her nose a second time.

"I..." Becky was flustered. "You're teasing me."

"Nope. I knew you were worth fighting for the moment you looked at me over the top of your glasses." He winked and offered her a smile. "I had one of those naughty librarian fantasies and it needed exploring."

"What?"

"The fantasy about the button-down, highly intellectual, sexually repressed woman who hides a smoldering sensuality." He held her chin. "Guess I was right about you from the start."

She gave him a playful swat.

"You've starred in lots of my fantasies, but the naughty librarian is the only one I can tell you about in polite company."

Becky swallowed, recalling a few of her own fantasies regarding Will. They were definitely X-rated.

He kissed his way from her forehead down her nose to her mouth, then across her cheek to her earlobe. She giggled, loving the fact that he kept kissing her, as though he couldn't get enough of her.

"Tell me about your other fantasies." She gasped when he nipped the side of her throat.

Will gazed into her eyes. "All right, but I'd rather we continued this discussion in the bedroom. Naked," he said, lifting her into his arms and carrying her up the stairs as if she weighed nothing. "Because you're a woman who should be made love to and often, Scarlett, and by someone who knows how."

"Oh." Becky brought her hand to her chest. "I seem to be having one of my Rhett-Butler-ravishes-Scarlett fantasies."

Will rewarded her with a huge grin. "Why, Miss Scarlett. Ah do believe you've shocked me. A young lady like you, havin' *fantasies.*"

She laughed, feeling completely at ease. "I have a confession to make. I fell in love with your dimples that first day in court." She touched a fingertip to one as he lowered her to the bed.

"Now, Scarlett," he said as he reached for the hem of her sweater. "You know ol' Rhett doesn't have sissy things like dimples."

He stripped off her sweater and bra and tossed them behind him. His shirt followed. Becky laughed. This was some fantasy and she was eager to play along.

Soft moonlight filtered through the curtains, outlining Will's body. He was magnificent.

He kissed each wrist, then pinned her hands above her head, making her feel totally exposed and vulnerable.

She loved this role-playing of characters so different from themselves. Rhett Butler, the ultimate alpha male, and Scarlett, the beautiful, frivolous seductress. Secretly, Becky had always wanted to be more like Scarlett. Will was offering her the chance.

With his free hand, he stroked her, his eyes following his hand's slow progress down over her throat, between her breasts, across her abdomen. She swallowed.

He trailed his hand lower, over her jeans….

Needing to feel his skin against hers, have him caress her in places no man had touched for so long, she struggled to release her hands from his grip but he held her fast and teased her some more.

"Oh, my…Scarlett, these seem to be rather thick pantalets you're wearin' today," he said in a deep, gravelly voice, then bent to kiss her.

She used the distraction to pull her hands from his grasp and undo the top button of her jeans.

Will ran a finger up and down her zipper, taunting her.

"Scarlett, what's this here newfangled contraption you have in your pantalets?" he asked and lowered his head to undo her zipper—with his teeth.

She gasped as his hot breath brushed against her, then she lifted her hips and took her jeans and panties off in one smooth motion. She wanted Will so much she couldn't wait another moment. "Now," she whimpered.

"Scarlett, my dear, you be a good girl and just wait till ol' Rhett has had his wicked way with you," he said and kissed her bare tummy. When he poked his wet tongue into her belly button, Becky collapsed in a boneless heap, surrendering to his mastery.

She combed her hand through his hair, savoring the softness of it and the delicious sensation of his mouth moving lower. And when he spread her thighs and began to taste her, sending flares of ecstasy arcing through her body, she nearly wept.

"Why…Rhett," she said, her voice breathless.

"Hush, Scarlett," he murmured.

Will had a very clever tongue, she decided as the delicious sensations spiraled, intensified and exploded into waves of exquisite pleasure.

When she finally recovered her senses, he was hovering over her wearing a huge grin.

"Did you find that mighty pleasin', Miss Scarlett?"

"Oh, Rhett," she cooed in her best southern-belle accent, lifting the back of her hand to her brow as if to ward off a faint. "I can't think about that raht now. If I do, I'll go crazy. I'll think about it tomorrow."

"Tomorrow could be a long way off with what I've got planned for tonight, my dear," he said, pretending to twirl his mustache, a lascivious look in his eye.

"*Sir,* you are no gentleman," she told him in a stern Scarlett voice. "Now get up, you varmint, and let me have *my* way."

BECKY AWOKE in the afterglow of a night's lovemaking. It had been intense. Beautiful. Will was everything she could have wished for in a lover, and so much more.

She'd made herself vulnerable by putting her trust in someone else so completely and been repaid with the most precious gift.

She rolled over to gaze at him. Will lay on his back, his arms flung over his head, the sheets pushed down, scarcely covering his nakedness. A smile curved her lips as she described him in one word: *potent.*

She pulled the sheet up to cover him in the early-morning cold. Will seemed to like sleeping with hardly any bedding and she liked to snuggle under the blankets. That was something they'd have to work out in the future—

She sat up. Her sudden indrawn breath woke him.

"What's up?"

She turned away, reached for her robe and drew it on. Will tugged at her hand and pulled her back down on the bed.

"I asked what's wrong?"

"Who said anything's wrong?" she replied, unable to face him.

"Look at me," he commanded.

Wrapping her robe tightly across her breasts, Becky forced herself to face him. The man was magnificent, she thought. *But they didn't have a future.*

He leaned on one elbow, the muscles of his chest taut, his biceps tensed, a frown creasing his brow.

"Sweetheart?" He reached for her but she flinched away, then cursed herself for being so transparent.

"I take it this is your manifestation of the 'morning after'?" he asked, sitting up and scrubbing at his face. Then his eyes bore into her. "Despite what you said last night, you're having regrets."

"Of course not," she answered and turned away, before he read the lie in her eyes. What was she *thinking* last night when she'd invited him in? She'd let her guard down, succumbed to her growing feelings for him and, in doing so, had crossed the boundary between employer and employee. She'd *used* him.

If she couldn't be trusted to make judgments about her personal life, what hope did she have in making judgments on the lives of others?

"Yeah. You *are* having regrets. Big ones," he said bluntly.

Becky could hear the disappointment in his voice. When she felt him get out of bed, a deep emptiness filled her heart.

"I'm sorry, but I can't help feeling this way."

"Precisely what way is that?" He'd come around the bed to stand in front of her. Naked.

Becky averted her eyes. "For one foolish moment…I let my body rule my head. The whole town will find out about this and, once they do, so will everyone who matters in Denver."

"What the *hell* are you saying?" he demanded, grasping her chin and forcing her to look into his eyes. They blazed black and furious.

"You're my employee. You've been a defendant in my court. You don't even have a real job—"

"What?"

"You can't deny that. Any of it. Once it gets out that we spent the night together—and knowing how small-town grapevines work, that won't be long—I won't be able to hold my head up in public and I'll never get appointed to a better position back in Denver."

"You're *ashamed* of me?"

"What? No!" She threw up her hands in exasperation. "I'm angry with myself. I can't believe I was so *stupid*."

Will paced to the other side of the room. She watched, mesmerized by his masculine beauty, her heart breaking with the certain knowledge that she couldn't both have the job she craved *and* Will. They were mutually exclusive.

He snatched up his jeans and pulled them on, buttoning them as he glared at her.

At least he was now partly clothed. She couldn't talk to him while he was naked. He was too exposed physically and she felt too exposed emotionally.

"For a start," he said as he returned to the bed, "I'm not going to be taking out an ad announcing that we're lovers."

"But—"

"No!" He cut her off. "You've had your say, and now you

can listen to me." He paced the room again, yanking his hand through his hair in a gesture of frustration. He turned back to her. "Despite what you think, no one in this town cares about our private business and anyone who does is irrelevant. Same for anyone in Denver." He turned back to her and demanded, "Are you ashamed of being seen with me?"

"No, of course not! I already told you that."

"You figure because I don't have a 'job'—" he held up his fingers and drew quotation marks around the word "—that I'm beneath you?"

Becky was slower to answer this time and Will jumped on it. "That about says it all, then, doesn't it?"

"I didn't mean it like that."

"Really? Then exactly how *did* you mean it?" He raised his hand when she started to answer. "No, save it. You're regretting that you slept with a ski bum who's appeared before you in court *and* happens to be your employee. Well, you can cross one of those off the list, because I quit!"

"You can't do that! What about Nicolas?"

"I didn't say I was quitting on Nick. I just quit the job. The one where you pay me to sleep with you."

"You know that's not true!"

"Save it, Your *Honor.*" He stalked to the bedroom door and hauled it open. "I really thought you cared about me, that you trusted me and we had a future together—"

Becky couldn't believe what she was hearing. "A *future?* In *this* town?" she blurted.

He leaned against the door frame. "You hate this town, don't you? You hate that you took the job here. You hate thinking everyone knows everyone else's business. Hell! You probably even hate it because people are friendly. Well, here's a reality check for you, *sweetheart*—you won't find a better place anywhere to live in and raise a child. You won't find better people to be your neighbors and friends and, yes, stand before you in court.

"And you will *never* find a man who will love you the way I do!" he roared, then stormed out of the room, slamming the door.

Chapter Nineteen

She couldn't move. Couldn't breathe.

Had Will said he loved her?

No one, apart from Nicolas, had ever told her that. Not her parents. Not her ex-husband. Yet Will had said it and with such passion.

Something akin to joy bloomed in her chest, then was quickly replaced by panic.

Oh, God, what have I done? she railed at herself as she pulled on her clothes, raced downstairs and tore open the front door.

The world outside looked like a Christmas card. Snow covered everything in a pure white blanket. *You won't find a better place anywhere to live and raise a child.*

Will was right, she thought as she glanced across the street to the tiny Episcopalian church, painted a cheery yellow and trimmed in white, its steeple reaching to the sky. Next to that was a Victorian cottage, painted in a soft blue and trimmed in salmon, and next to that, a run-down relic of the mining years, all rusted corrugated tin and bare timber slab walls brimming with rustic character and charm. Her neighbors on either side of her dwelled in homes filled with warmth and love. The neighborhood was quiet, peaceful. Safe. It was like a scene from a Norman Rockwell painting.

About to throw on her coat and go in search of Will, she

noticed that the snow on her front path hadn't been disturbed. He must still be in the house. "Will!" she cried, closing the front door and heading for kitchen.

He was leaning against the countertop, glaring at her. It had all become so clear—he was hurting and she loved him and that was all that mattered.

She ran to him and flung her arms around his neck. "I love you. Please don't go. I'm sorry for everything I said. I was *so* wrong. Please forgive me."

His hands clasped hers to release her stranglehold and for one dreadful moment she thought he'd thrust her away, tell her it was too late, that she'd had her one and only chance and blown it.

His dark eyes raked her face. She probably looked terrible, but she didn't care. Will was about to walk out the door and out of her life and she was going to do everything she could to make him stay.

"What did you say?" he demanded, his look no less severe, his hands gripping hers, hard and unyielding.

"I'm sorry."

"Before that," he said through clenched teeth.

She studied his face, unable to remember everything she'd blubbered, but she did remember one thing. "I love you."

His eyes narrowed and his lips thinned as he considered her words. "Do you mean it?"

"Yes!" she answered without hesitation. "You're right. This is the perfect town to raise a child. I was so focused on my career, on my need to secure a well-paid job to ensure my son's future, that I couldn't see what's been staring me in the face all along." She paused and took a deep breath, then said, "I don't ever want to be without you, Will."

The side of his mouth turned up. "Do I need to ask you to swear to that in a court of law?"

Her heart soared. He wasn't going to leave! He didn't hate her for what she'd said. Such careless, *stupid,* insensitive words! "I'll swear it to the entire audience of the courthouse come tomorrow if you like."

"You would?"

"Yes, absolut—"

Becky's declaration was cut off when he covered her mouth in a searing kiss that had every nerve in her body singing with joy. His big hands clasped her face so tenderly and she returned his passion, gasping as Will nuzzled the side of her throat. The scratchiness of his morning whiskers sent heat licking through her body. When his mouth moved lower to bite gently at the swell of her breast through the fabric of her sweater, the sensations were exquisite. Carnal.

"Make love to me," she said, but Will stepped back and took her hands.

"I don't need to remind you what happened this morning."

"It won't happen again."

"It might." He released her hands and strode to the other side of the kitchen before turning toward her. "It kills me to say this, but I think we need to cool it for a bit."

"What?"

HER EYES GLOWED with green spears of anger, and Will couldn't help grinning at her indignant expression and her petulant pout. He felt warmed by the knowledge she wanted him so badly.

Much as he wished he could drag Becky back upstairs, now wasn't the time. One of them needed to keep a cool head about this, and she had to get ready for work.

A HALF HOUR LATER she was back downstairs, dressed immaculately, not a hair out of place and with no trace of the night's lovemaking. She pulled on her gloves and said, "Please explain what you meant by 'cool it for a bit.'"

"I think we should step back for a while—at least until Nick returns to school."

"What difference does that make?"

He could hear the frustration in her voice. It mirrored his own. The scene in her bedroom earlier had cut him to the quick.

Becky might want to protect her heart from ever being hurt again. But he needed to protect *his* heart, too.

"When Nick goes back to school, I'll no longer be his full-time caregiver, and therefore not your employee. Then our relationship will be on a more even footing."

"But I'll still need you to collect him from school and help with his homework. I can't do this on my own, Will. I *need* you! Nicolas needs you."

He helped her into her coat. "I'll be there for you. I won't let you down. But I won't be your employee anymore."

"I don't understand. Either you work for me looking after Nick—or what?"

"I do it for free. I do it as a friend."

"Seems to be a very one-sided friendship to me. What do you get out of it? I can't return the favor."

"You can let me date you."

Becky gave a snort of disbelief. "I think after last night we've moved past needing to date."

"I don't agree. The fact that you felt you'd put your reputation at risk is all the more reason for us to cool it. I don't ever again want to wake up and see the look in your eyes I saw this morning. I'm in this relationship for the long-term, Becky. Not a one-night stand."

"I can't believe you're even speaking to me. I've treated you abominably." Her face was flushed. "I'm sorry."

"I aim to prove to you that you *can* be good at relationships—fulfilling ones that will last a lifetime."

"Look, just because I admitted I love you doesn't mean I want to marry you!"

"You will," he said with utter conviction.

Chapter Twenty

"Have you seen today's paper?" Those were his mother's first words once Will had snatched up the insistently ringing phone the following morning.

"Mom?" He sat up groggily and rubbed his face. "What's up?"

"Get yourself out of bed and find a paper," Sarah said, her voice holding uncharacteristic panic. "Becky's in trouble!"

Will scrambled out of bed, hauled on his jeans and sweater and went downstairs to the free newsstand outside Mrs. C.'s shop.

He flipped through it and there on page seven, for all the world to see, was a photograph of him and Becky and the headline blaring *Judge Shows Bias Toward Lover's Protest Movement.* Will felt as though he'd been hit in the chest.

The photographer had caught them in an intimate moment at the Christmas carol ceremony. Becky had wrapped a scarf around his neck, and for a moment their eyes had held. He'd been tempted to kiss her, but she'd blushed and looked away. Fortunately, he hadn't given in to his impulse, otherwise the photograph would've been far more damaging.

He frowned. Until now, the paper had thrown its unconditional support behind saving the buildings. He needed to warn Becky about the article before she went to work.

BECKY'S EYES NARROWED as she scanned the story. "This is libelous," she murmured, then pointed to a heading in tiny font at the top of the full-page story. "It's an advertisement taken out by the development company. And there's a disclaimer from the paper—see?"

Will cursed. "I was in such a hurry to get over here, I didn't notice. But it's still potentially dangerous for you. I wonder who placed it."

"I should think that's obvious." A smile curved her lips.

"What are you grinning about? Your reputation's been smeared all over the paper! It says you're biased toward the protest group because you're sleeping with me!"

"The court records will prove that I didn't show any bias toward your case. You presented a very reasonable argument, so I granted the injunction." She laughed and said, "I'd *love* to be a fly on the wall when Jason Whitby sees this!"

"Ah, hello?" Will waved his hand in front of her eyes. "Care to share the funny part with me?"

"The development company, through their PR bungling, has slandered me. And you."

"But we *are* lovers. Or were, for one night," he reminded her.

"They have no proof of that. I'm going to sue the backsides off those jerks!" she declared and turned to Will, her eyes alight. "By printing this garbage, they've exposed themselves. By trying to ruin my reputation and discredit you, and therefore regain support for developing the site, they've made a huge mistake. It puts you in a very good negotiating position to buy back the buildings." She chuckled. "Jason Whitby's going to freak when he reads this!"

"I'd better call Mom. She's worried for you."

"Let me call her in that case. I'll explain everything and set her mind at ease."

With Sarah mollified and offering her utmost support, Becky headed off to the courthouse. She had some work to do for herself this morning, starting libel proceedings against the development company. She rubbed her hands together, enthusiastic about taking charge of her career and her future. There was no way she was going to let anyone get away with maligning her character and disparaging her decisions.

SHORTLY BEFORE NINE, Becky pressed the send button on an e-mail to Jason Whitby, then entered the courtroom for the morning's session.

At 9:05, a message was passed to her. Jason Whitby wanted to speak to her *urgently.*

She returned to her case. Jason Whitby could wait.

There was a larger-than-usual audience and Becky surmised that many had come to see if she'd make a public statement.

During her first recess, Whitby called again—apparently he'd been calling every few minutes. At first he tried his smarmy lawyer approach, flattering her, apologizing profusely for his client's stupid mistake, begging her forgiveness.

Becky enjoyed hearing him debase himself, then cut him off midsentence. "Mr. Whitby! In future you can communicate with me through my lawyer."

At the interruption, he turned nasty, threatening her with dire consequences to her career if she didn't drop the suit. At any other time, a threat like that would have Becky seriously thinking of backing down, but her ire was up and she was out for blood.

"You wouldn't by any chance be making a direct threat to a judge of the Colorado courts, would you?" she snapped.

"No, of course not, Becky, er, Judge. I merely wanted to warn you that you were in an untenable position."

"I think you should be using those words to your client."

"Oh, come on! Surely we can do a deal that protects your reputation and my client's. You don't want the sordid details of your affair with a defendant splashed all over the Denver papers, do you?"

And now he'd returned to form. He was so predictable. "For a start, there is nothing *sordid* going on between me and Will O'Malley. I employed him as a caregiver for my son during the holidays. If you want to make a big deal out of a male taking that role, then bring it on. I'd be only too happy to point out that this is a small town and it was difficult to find suitably qualified caregivers. I'd also point out what a remarkable difference I've seen in my *disabled—*" Becky put the emphasis on the word, although she hated to use it to further her ends "—son, during the short time Will O'Malley has been caring for him. I'm sure you'd like to take on all the groups that represent people with disabilities and tell them just who *is* and who is *not* suitable to care for their children."

"There's the photo—"

"*What* photo? The one with me smiling at a joke Will made?"

"It looks like you're smiling at more than that."

Becky sighed to indicate she was bored with their conversation. "If you say so. I've wasted enough time talking to you. I'll have my lawyer contact you." She hung up, grinning with glee. Now she needed a lawyer. Someone local would be perfect and would send the message that she had nothing to hide, nothing to defend. Using a big-city lawyer of Jason Whitby's ilk might suggest otherwise.

Mike Cochrane had recently moved back to Spruce Lake and was looking for clients. She liked his easygoing yet competent manner. After putting a call through to his office, she returned to the courtroom.

But as the next session got under way, the courtroom gradually cleared. Becky noticed that a note was being passed among the audience and was tempted to ask what was going on.

By lunchtime, the audience consisted only of family members of the defendants.

Her phone rang as she entered her office. Tempted to let it ring, since she didn't need any more grief from Jason Whitby, she instead snatched it up and barked, "*What?*"

"Whoa, there!"

Becky relaxed at the sound of Will's voice. "I'm sorry," she said with a smile, picturing him. "Can we start again?"

"If you're having a bad day, Judge, then I suggest you take a lunchtime walk down to the old buildings."

She decided to do just that. Ten minutes later, Becky was having trouble getting through to the site, as the street was jammed with honking vehicles and outside-broadcast vans from Denver and national television networks.

There was a staccato roar. She couldn't make out what was being said, but the placards carried by nearly everyone told the story.

Hands Off Our Buildings!

Hands Off Our Judge!

Take Your Dirty Tricks and Stick Them Where the Sun…

Becky didn't need to read the rest of that one, carried by Frank Farquar. Louella wore a sign around her neck. Becky was trying to read it when Will spotted her and made his way through the crowd, his face glowing with joy. "What do you think of *this* protest?" he asked.

"Overwhelming," she said with a grin and pointed to the signs. "Were you responsible for these?"

"I wish I could take the credit, but most of them were done by Miss P. and the folks at the Twilight Years."

Becky spotted several seniors in the placard-carrying group.

"The article has really brought people out in support of you." Will gestured at more signs. Our Judge Fights Fair! Dirty Developers No Match for Honorable Judge. Spruce Lake Supports Judge Becky!

Becky couldn't stop the smile spreading across her face. "Oh, my," she finally murmured.

Several protestors saw her standing on the edge of the crowd and a cheer went up. The television cameras swung her way. Being the center of attention was not what she wanted.

A microphone was shoved into her face and a reporter asked, "Judge McBride, what was your reaction to the piece in this morning's local paper?"

She managed to swallow the lump in her throat and said, "The protest to save the old buildings on this site has brought out the very best in people, and the very worst in others." She bit her tongue, not mentioning the mayor, Jason Whitby and anyone who wanted to destroy the heritage of this very special town. "I'm grateful for the support of the people of Spruce

Lake. This is a wonderful, caring community and I shall continue to serve the citizens of Spruce Lake to the best of my ability until my term ends in a few months."

A barrage of questions from other journalists followed, but Will insinuated himself between them and Becky, effectively protecting her. He took over, allowing Becky to slip away, back to the courthouse.

She concentrated on breathing in the fresh mountain air and replayed the sight of the protest in her head, feeling a tiny thrill at the community's support. It also helped her come to a few decisions regarding her future and Spruce Lake.

Back in her chambers, she put through a call to Judge Stevens. By the time she'd finished, Mike Cochrane was waiting to see her.

"JUDGE MCBRIDE?" Her assistant interrupted Becky's thoughts as she wound down from the afternoon session. "Will O'Malley's on the line."

Smiling, Becky picked up the phone and was assailed by noise and cheering. She could barely hear Will above it.

"Get your glad rags on, Your Honor, we're celebrating tonight!"

"What's going on?"

"The development company is pulling out *and* they want to sell us the buildings!"

"That's wonderful, Will! Congratulations."

There was a pause. "I'm sorry about the article in the paper. It tipped everything in our favor. But I feel bad for you."

"Don't. I've had quite an eventful day and come to a few decisions regarding my future."

"I hope it includes me?"

"We'll see," she said enigmatically.

"Oh, the judge is teasing me," he said, and she could hear the amusement in his voice. "Care to join us all at Rusty's for a celebratory drink?"

"Just try and keep me away. Where's Nicolas?"

"Right here beside me. Sash and Daisy, too. They're on to

their second round of root-beer floats. I'm amazed the little guy hadn't tried one till I took him to Rusty's the day school ended."

Becky experienced a pang of regret at all the things other kids probably took for granted and Nicolas had missed out on. All of that was going to change!

"I'll meet you there in fifteen minutes," she said and hung up the phone.

RUSTY'S WAS NEARLY BURSTING at the seams when Becky pushed through the door. A rousing cheer went up when the crowd became aware of her arrival.

Will bounded up to her. Becky was afraid he might kiss her in front of everyone, but he seemed mindful of the television cameras present and instead clasped her hand and shook it.

"I'm the one who should be shaking *your* hand," she yelled above the din as Will drew her away to a quieter corner of the bar. "When I first met you in court, I didn't think you and your protest group would have a snowflake's chance in hell of getting the development company to back down. The fact that they've also agreed to sell to you is quite a coup, Will. Well done."

He grinned and leaned close. "You can kiss me later." He leaned back again and frowned as he examined her face. "You look different. What's going on?"

"I've made a few decisions regarding my future."

"You dodged giving me any details when I phoned. Fess up." Will took a long draft of beer, then put the bottle on the bar and braced his arm against the wall behind her.

"Okay, if you must know, I called Judge Stevens this afternoon."

Will stiffened. "You're leaving?"

Placing her hand on his chest, she could feel the strong beat of his heart beneath her palm and it gave her strength. "No, I'm staying."

Will grinned. He was about to say something but she held up her hand.

"When Judge Stevens returns to work, we're going to job

share. She's enjoying being a mom too much to want to return to work full-time. But she does want to work. So we've figured out this scenario, pending official approval. That way I can spend more time with Nicolas. I've missed too much of his childhood already and I don't want to miss any more. I can live here very comfortably on a part-time judge's salary."

"But you had your heart set on a promotion in Denver."

"I did. But the events of the past few days and a few things your mom said at the barbecue have made me rethink what I really want from life, and it isn't power, position or even money. I want to be happy and I want Nicolas to be happy and have friends. I think I've found where I want to spend the rest of my life."

Will's face broke into the broadest grin. He was about to pull her into his arms, but once again she put a staying hand on his chest.

"I want to say something before you congratulate me on realizing what's really important in life."

"O...kay." His agreement was measured.

"I don't want you to feel pressured in any way. You're not obligated to date me or spend time with me or Nicolas just because we're going to be permanent residents of the town. I'd hate it if you ended up resenting me or feeling that having me around is cramping your need for freedom, to be yourself. To...date other women."

"Are you kidding? Sweetheart, I *want* to be with you! This is the best news I've had all day. It even trumps the development company pulling out." He hauled her into his arms and kissed her long and hard.

"Am I interrupting anything?"

Matt's voice did indeed interrupt something, but Becky was grateful. She was also grateful the rest of the bar couldn't see her and Will locked in their embrace, since Matt was blocking anyone's view.

"Come and join the party, you two, before those cameras find you slinking around in dark corners," he said.

There was much handshaking and backslapping as the bar swelled with more well-wishers, and Will related to his parents and to Becky the reason for the development company's turnaround. "Their official line is that in the face of such well-organized opposition, they didn't see any growth worth pursuing in the town in the foreseeable future." He rolled his eyes. "The unofficial line is that they overstepped the mark, assumed they could walk all over the citizens of a small town, destroy its heritage and defame their judge—" he pulled Becky close "—and get away with it. The delays incurred by further protests and a pending lawsuit meant it wasn't fiscally prudent for them to stay in the town."

Becky smiled to herself. She'd tell Will later how she and Mike Cochrane had struck a deal with the development company. She'd drop the lawsuit if they agreed to sell the buildings back for what they'd paid for them. The development company was only too glad to get out of Spruce Lake, since their public profile had taken such a battering. They'd wanted to make a profit, but Mike had stood his ground and convinced them any profits they stood to make would be swallowed up in a further lawsuit, and their reputations would be irreparably damaged as a result. By midafternoon, the deal had been struck.

The protestors had won their fight, with a little help from Becky.

Looking around at the happy faces at Rusty's, she felt her heart ache. Although the O'Malleys had made her and Nicolas feel welcome at their family gatherings, she didn't *belong* here. Not yet, anyway. She didn't know how to put down roots that would go deep enough to be permanent and bonds that would never break, no matter how difficult the hardship, no matter how testing the circumstances. She'd never had the opportunity to be part of anything really worthwhile—apart from her relationship with Nicolas.

But Becky knew she wanted *this,* wanted to feel a sense of belonging, to someone, to a community. All evening, she was intensely aware of Will beside her.

"Kiss me," he murmured, while the crowd sang, appropriately enough, "O, Little Town of Bethlehem." His hand cupped her chin, turning her face toward his.

"I don't—" she began, interrupted when Will's mouth covered hers, warding off all conscious thought. Her only awareness was of Will's lips on hers, and, oh, they felt so good. He brushed his lips over hers, then deepened the kiss.

When the crowd cheered, they sprang apart like a pair of schoolkids caught making out behind the gymnasium. Becky could feel herself blushing. She looked around. Everyone was smiling—even Luke O'Malley.

So much for keeping what was happening with her and Will a secret!

She glanced over at Nicolas sitting in a booth with Luke's daughters and Miss Patterson. He held up his hand, his thumb and forefinger joined in an okay sign as he beamed from ear to ear.

"I'VE GOT AN APPOINTMENT at the bank tomorrow," Will said as they walked home together. Nicolas, at Sarah's insistence, was spending the night at the ranch.

It had started snowing. Fat, lazy flakes drifted down, and Becky decided it was her favorite type of snow. She loved walking in it and would always associate it with Christmas in the Colorado Rockies.

"I'm arranging a loan to buy back the old buildings, using my ranch land as collateral. They've generously agreed to let me develop the land myself, rather than having to sell it off to someone else." He put his arm around her shoulders, squeezing her closer. "I get to write the covenants, and the wildlife will be protected. It's turned out better than I could've hoped."

She kissed his cheek, no longer caring who saw them or what they thought about it. "You've done a wonderful job."

"Why, thank you, ma'am." Will offered her a deep bow, then straightened. "Although I think the development company shooting themselves in the foot helped speed matters up." He bent to scoop up some snow and attempted to fashion it into a ball, but the snow was too dry to stick and it fell apart.

"I have people wanting to be tenants of the old buildings once they're restored. Others want to buy into the condos and houses." He shook his head in astonishment. "I can't believe how fast word has spread about the plans for the site. I suspect Jack's been doing some campaigning of his own. Frank told me tonight he's moving back to town and wants one of the Victorian houses. I have it on good authority that Lou and Charles approve of the move."

Becky smiled at the vision of Louella lounging on the front porch of a Victorian home. "I'm delighted he and Edna seem to have put their differences aside. I saw them sharing a booth tonight and they looked very contented in each other's company."

Will nodded. "Maybe we should be thanking the development company, after all."

"How do you figure that?"

"For a start, we wouldn't have met, which means I might never have met Nick and you wouldn't have adopted Dugald. Frank and Edna wouldn't have had the protest movement to throw them together. I wouldn't have found out what an astute investor I was all those years ago— Hey!" he protested as Becky punched his arm lightly. He grabbed her elbows and tugged her toward him. "And I wouldn't have found a job that interests me enough to stay in the town."

"You have a job?"

"Well, duh!" he said with a smile. "Who do you think is going to be the project manager of all these renovations?"

"You?"

Will pretended outrage. "Well, of course me! I'm not completely hopeless."

"I never said you were. But project managing seems a very disciplined thing to do and, until recently, they wouldn't be traits I'd have attributed to your character."

He grinned. "You've got a point."

"However, you've displayed tremendous organizational

skills and tenacity with the protest movement. I'm sure with your dedication to saving and preserving those buildings, it can't help but be a success."

He grinned. "Jack'll do an incredible job converting those buildings. He's already lining up subcontractors."

"I'm looking forward to seeing his plans. There's so much you can do with those Victorian homes."

Will whispered in her ear, "And I'm looking forward to showing you what I can do in your Victorian bedroom."

He hoisted Becky in his arms and carried her the rest of the way home.

SO MUCH FOR COOLING IT, she thought with a smile as she lay spooned against Will later that night.

Chapter Twenty-one

Will put on coffee for breakfast, then pulled the kitchen curtains aside. Christmas Eve, and it was still snowing. Nick would get his Christmas wish.

The landscape looked serene, but high up in the mountains the snow would be piling up and turning into something potentially lethal. He moved away from the window.

"I'm meeting with the bank at midday to arrange the loan," he told Becky as she scrambled eggs for them both.

"I planned on taking Nick skiing," Will continued, "and then he can join the ski-school kids during their lunch break. Is that okay with you? He'll be safe there and can tag on to a class if I'm not back in time. It'll be a good chance for him to try a few things without me hovering over him. At the moment, I think he only believes he can ski because I'm there with him."

Becky looked up from her task and smiled. "I'm sure he doesn't believe that at all and of course it's fine with me."

"I'LL BE BACK AS SOON as the meeting's over, little buddy," Will told Nick as he walked him into the ski-school hut after their morning lesson.

Another thunderous boom echoed from high up in the mountains, and Will steeled himself against the familiar sound of the avalanche blasting that had gone on throughout the morning. The snow had let up not long after they'd arrived at the slopes.

Nick had been pressuring him to go up on the four-person chairlift that took them higher than the protected kiddie slopes. Will had steadfastly refused.

They found Tom Schilling, one of the children's ski-school instructors, who greeted him, saying, "Go buy those buildings before the development company changes its mind, Will!"

Will squatted down to Nick's level. "Are you sure you don't mind staying here while I go to the bank?"

Nick gave Will one of his uninhibited hugs. "I'll be fine! It'll be fun not having you nagging at me all the time." He softened the comment with a grin. "Good luck, Will. Hey, I'm proud of you."

Nick was proud of him. That meant a lot. A heck of a lot. His voice was husky when he said, "Thanks, champ. I'm proud of you, too."

NICOLAS HAD FINISHED LUNCH and slipped outside to play in the snow with some of the other kids while they waited for their afternoon lesson when he heard someone calling him. "Hey, Nick!"

He glanced toward the caller. It was Johnny Cooper with a group of his friends. He wanted to ignore them and work on his snowman, but Will had talked to Johnny and they'd shaken hands on being friends. It would be rude to ignore him, so he said, "Hi. You having a good time?"

"Sure! What about you?"

"Great," Nicolas said and then, wanting to impress Johnny, said, "I'm going up on the kiddie chair later."

"Cool! Hey, wanna come up with me and my friends now?"

Nicolas looked in Tom Schilling's direction. He was talking to some younger kids.

"C'mon, Nick! I saw you skiing before and you're real good. Those turns you were doin' were *dy-na-mite.*"

That excited Nicolas. "Really?"

"Yeah. So, c'mon. We're gonna ride the kiddie chair now. You can ride with me. Be my buddy."

Nicolas had never been anyone's buddy before. Except Will's, of course, but not another kid's.

He had to get permission first. He walked over to Tom, who was demonstrating the snowplow position to one of the children.

"Hey, Tom. Some of my friends from school are here and want me to go on the kiddie chair with them. Can I?"

Tom looked over at the group. They all smiled and waved back. Tom shrugged. "Sure, but stay where I can see you, okay? Class starts again in thirty minutes."

"Okay!" Nicolas cried and went to join Johnny.

They rode up in the kiddie chair a couple of times and Johnny told jokes the whole way. Johnny and his friends were really good skiers and gave him a few tips. Then Johnny said, "You wanna come up in the big chairlift with us?"

Nicolas hesitated and glanced at Tom. He was still involved with the little kids. "I dunno. I was supposed to stay here. My class starts soon."

"Aw, c'mon, you don't want anyone thinking you're a baby, do you?"

"Well, no," Nicolas agreed. He really wanted to go higher up the mountain.

"C'mon," Johnny urged. "I saw those O'Malley girls up there earlier. We can go find them and be back before he even notices you're gone." He indicated Tom.

Sasha and Daisy were on the mountain? Nicolas wanted to show them what he'd learned. Maybe he could ski with them? "Okay," he said and followed Johnny and his friends onto the bigger chairlift.

FIFTEEN MINUTES LATER, Nicolas wasn't so sure going with Johnny was a good idea, even if Sasha and Daisy were up here somewhere. Johnny had said they'd get off at the first chairlift. But then they'd all skied over and boarded another lift to go higher. Not wanting to be left alone and not knowing his way down the mountain, Nicolas had followed.

Then they'd caught the T-bar. Johnny had helped Nicolas

onto it, and the next thing he knew, he was being whisked farther up the mountain. Johnny pointed out White Cloud Bowl as they rode higher and higher.

Fear clawed at Nicolas's throat. He wanted to go back down. There were no trees up here and the mountain looked spooky. His legs felt unsteady on the T-bar and he was terrified of falling off. He clung to the bar like a drowning person clinging to a life raft.

He wanted to get off, but the sides of the T-bar trail fell away sharply on each side. "I…I want to go back," he said as they neared the top.

"Scared?" Nicolas didn't like the challenge in Johnny's eyes.

"N-no…but Tom told me to stay where he could see me."

Johnny sighed as though he was disappointed in him. "I brought you up here 'cause you said you wanted to ski from the top of the mountain."

"I…d-do." Nicolas's fear was increasing by the minute. This place was far too forbidding. "But I…I want to go back down now," he said as the T-bar was wrenched out from under him.

"The only way down is to ski," Johnny stated as they skied off to the side of the unloading area.

The mountain was nearly vertical! "I…I can't ski—" he swallowed "—that."

"Sure you can. I do it all the time," Johnny boasted.

"B-but I c-can't."

Johnny sighed again. "Okay, then we'll have to take the easy way down. Come on." He skied off along a less steep path.

They got to an area with a rope across it and a sign saying Area Closed—Avalanche Danger!

Avalanche! Nicolas's blood froze. This was *not* a good place to be.

Johnny and his buddies slipped under the rope.

"Wait!" he called. "It says the area's closed."

Johnny looked back at him. "They have that sign up there all the time. It doesn't mean anything."

Nicolas glanced behind him. They'd dropped in elevation.

It would be a hard climb to get back to the run Nicolas had noticed over on the other side of the T-bar. He'd seen skiers getting off it and skiing in the other direction.... He wished he'd followed those people instead of Johnny.

He glanced over at Johnny and his buddies. The bowl looked awfully steep and sinister. But Johnny said it was the only way down.

"C'mon!" he yelled. "We're freezing our butts off."

I can do this, Nicolas tried to reassure himself. *I can traverse over to the other side and back again lots of times to get down. And the snow looks soft...if I fall.*

Nicolas knew about traversing. Will had taught him the technique of skiing from one side of the slope to the other. He'd said you could get down a steep mountain if you did a *lot* of traversing. Okay...so he could get down this one. He just had to take it slowly. He set off, following Johnny and his buddies.

Three-quarters of the way across, he heard a shout and looked back. A ski patroller was coming toward them! Now he was really in trouble. Johnny and his buddies had already made several turns and were way below him.

A strange sound from above had him glancing up, his heart in his throat. The clouds hovering over the top of the bowl had opened to reveal a huge overhang—and it was cracking! Every nerve in his body froze as the cracks shot through the snowpack. Moments later, the overhanging snow gave up its struggle to stay attached to the mountain as gravity overtook it, and with an almighty *whumph* broke away and came rushing at him with an enormous white roar. It felt as though the world was moving in slow motion under his feet. Then it caught him up, accelerating at a frightening speed, consuming, choking, terrifying him as it tumbled him down the treacherous slope.

Panic-stricken, he cried out, but no one could hear him over the rumble of the avalanche as it tore down the mountain.

He struggled, trying to breaststroke, fighting for breath, fighting to reach the surface, thankful his skis had released. Will had talked to him about how to increase your chances of surviving an avalanche. He *had* to stay above the wave, but the forces were too strong and he was tumbled over again and again, catching glimpses of the sky beyond the swirling white wall of snow.

Snow filled his mouth. He spat it out and placed his hands over his face as the avalanche finally spent its fury. And then there was silence.

Snow pressed in around his body, against his chest and throat. He needed to breathe! He pushed his hands out, trying to create an air pocket, like Will had told him. Will was gonna be so mad when he found out he'd come up the mountain without him.

He needed to get to Will. To apologize for being so stupid. He tried to kick against the snow to get to the surface. But it had turned from harmless fluff to cement, packed hard around his legs.

He sobbed at the realization that he was buried beneath tons of snow and might never get out. Panic rose and consumed him as everything turned gray. Then black.

AFTER THE MEETING at the bank, Will headed back to the slopes. He and Becky had a lot to discuss this evening. Until he'd signed the contracts, he hadn't allowed himself to truly believe he had a future in Spruce Lake. But now he did. He owned something of significance—something worth preserving. And he'd fallen in love with a woman he'd walk to the ends of the earth for and a boy he already thought of as a son.

"Hey, Will, is Nick with you?"

Will glanced up at Tom Shilling's query. "I'm just back from my meeting," he managed to say despite the sickening sensation in his stomach. "Why did you think he was with me?"

"Some of his buddies came by and he asked if he could ski with them. I thought it'd be okay. They seemed friendly enough, and when he didn't come back I thought he'd met up with you."

"*What* buddies?"

"There were four of them. I recognized that kid Johnny Cooper."

Will felt as though an ice pick had been driven through his heart. Okay, so Nick and Johnny had shaken hands and were supposedly friends, but Will didn't trust Johnny an inch. He cursed himself for letting Nick think everything was all right so he'd have a stress-free Christmas.

His heart racing, he ran up the chairlift line, scanning the chairs and the slopes. When he couldn't spot him, he realized with nauseating certainty where Johnny would've taken Nick. To the one place Will was too scared to go—up the mountain!

He heard a deep rumbling from higher up, the vibrations rising through the soles of his ski boots as the noise increased, sounding like a runaway freight train roaring through the valley.

Will knew that sound only too well. A huge powder cloud filled the air, striking terror into his heart. It must be bad to be visible from down here.

"Avalanche!" he cried. "Get these kids to safety!" He started running uphill, searching for Nick, hoping he'd missed him among the dozens of kids on the slopes. Many of the children had stopped in their tracks, fear and confusion in their eyes. A few were crying for their mothers. Will didn't have time to comfort them. He had to find Nick.

THE COURTROOM WAS ABUZZ with rumors about an avalanche. Becky banged her gavel, trying to bring the court to order. All morning they'd heard the regular, deep *thwump, thwump* as the ski patrollers blasted potential avalanche zones. Several of the explosions were so intense they'd rattled the windows. However, this last one was different. This time the courtroom had seemed to shake.

The chatter finally settled down, but the fear Becky saw on the faces of the older residents sent shivers up her spine. This was bad. *Very* bad. She knew about the six skiers who'd skied out of bounds back in the 1980s and been killed by an avalanche. They were buried so deep their bodies weren't recovered until spring. The old-timers' anxiety was genuine and she needed to do something to alleviate it.

"I'm adjourning court for the rest of the day," she said and addressed the defendant. "Mr. Applegate, I'm dismissing the charges against you. But don't let me see you in my court for the same complaint next week, or I'll double the fine." She stood and left the courtroom, determined to discover what had happened.

WILL'S HEART THUMPED urgently. He'd never been so afraid in his life. Sirens were approaching from several directions. Police. Search and Rescue. Fire and Paramedics. Matt would be here soon. He'd know what to do. Matt never panicked.

The ski-school children had been ushered inside their meeting hut, where they'd be safe until their parents collected them. The mountain would be closed for the rest of the day while a search was mounted for anyone trapped in the avalanche.

Seeing Matt as he pulled up at the base of the lifts, Will raced over to him. "What's the official story?" he asked, pulling open his door.

Matt climbed out, his face showing lines of strain and worry that didn't relieve the panic rising in Will. "It's not good. Some kids were skiing out of bounds, and a couple of patrollers followed them under the ropes to bring them back. Before they got to them, the kids skied under a cornice and it slid."

"How many kids?"

"Does it matter? Look, I'm sorry, Will, but I can't talk right now, I've got to go."

"How many?" Will ground through teeth clenched to stop them from chattering with fear.

Matt sighed, clearly impatient. "Five."

Will couldn't control his mounting sense of unease. "I...I think Nick's up there."

"What?"

Will told him what he knew, ending the explanation with, "He went up with Johnny Cooper—the kid who's been terrorizing him. Johnny had three buddies with him."

Matt immediately called to the ski patrol. He turned to

Will, his expression grim. "There are two patrollers and five kids missing."

Panic and fear wrenched Will's gut. This was his fault. He shouldn't have let Nick believe things were okay with Johnny. "I'm going up there. I've got to find him."

Matt put a steadying hand on his arm. "You'll only get in the way. What if you freak out up there?"

Will shook him off. "I won't! I *have* to find Nick. And if some of the ski patrol is missing, they'll need everyone who knows about mountain rescue to help."

"If you freak out, you'll end up putting someone else's life in danger."

"Matt..."

"All right!" Matt hugged him, surprising Will. Matt never embraced him. Then he was businesslike again. "I'll let Becky know," he said, his voice hoarse.

Will nodded. "Break it to her gently, will you?"

Matt clapped him on the shoulder. "Of course. I'm trained to do this sort of thing, remember?"

WILL GOT HIS SKIS and strode to the chairlift loading area, where rescue teams were gathering. The ski-patrol headquarters located farther up the mountain would be in a frenzy of activity, too.

The slopes were clearing of skiers. Some who'd been waiting to board the lifts were shaking their heads at the news that people were trapped; others were grumbling about having their day's skiing spoiled.

He joined a group of rescue personnel, including Lloyd Wilmott.

"Will! Good to have you on board. You know the routine," Lloyd said and issued him a pack containing a shovel, walkie-talkie, crampons, lightweight emergency blanket, avalanche beacon, water and collapsible probes that could be extended to nine feet in length and pushed into the snow to search for buried victims.

As Will clicked into his skis, they were given a rundown on where the avalanche had occurred—up in White Cloud Bowl, an expanse of near-vertical walls of double-black diamond runs, high above the tree line. Only very advanced skiers—or the foolhardy—ever ventured there. The area was closed because of the heavy snowfalls of the past few days and the risk of avalanche. Now, the ski patrollers' worst nightmare—and Will's—had come true.

The ski patrollers were wearing beacons, so they should be located quickly. But Will, like the others around him, knew that beacons could fail, or be torn off, just as his was when he'd been caught in that monster avalanche in the Andes. Then it would be a race against time to locate and dig out the victims before they suffocated—or froze to death.

With his name checked off, Will prepared to board the chairlift. His heartbeat kicked up as he wiped away the perspiration beading his upper lip. He'd been running on adrenaline since the avalanche and during the briefing, but now the reality of going up the mountain hit him full force. He *had* to do this. He couldn't let them down. He had to do this—for Nick…and for himself.

Gritting his teeth, he slid into position. The chair caught him and swung a little, and Will gripped the safety bar as Craig, the rescuer sharing the chair, pulled it down.

"For a moment I thought you weren't going to get on, Will," the other man said.

Will smiled grimly. There was no going back now. He tried to concentrate on the beauty of the day. It was sunny and cloudless again. The clouds that had shrouded the mountain earlier had moved on. A perfect day, just like that last day in the Andes…

A whoop of joy spread down the chairlift. One of the patrollers had been found. His beacon had led the rescuers to him. However, the other patroller was still missing.

They changed lifts, and now he could see up into the bowl, something that wasn't possible from farther down. The devastation stretched right to the bottom of the bowl and beyond. Huge pines and spruce growing below the tree line had been knocked flat. Soon they were riding over the debris field, scattered with huge chunks of ice and snow.

Will closed his eyes, trying to remember the mountain the last time he'd been up here. Beautiful, perfect, pristine. It helped calm his racing heart, and when he opened his eyes again, he knew with clarity that finding Nick was the most important thing he would ever do in his life.

He made a silent vow. *I won't leave the mountain until every last skier's been brought out. Alive!*

Chapter Twenty-two

Becky's worst fears were realized when Matt strode into her chambers to report that victims were caught in the avalanche.

"Then why are you here, rather than up there helping?" she asked.

At the desolation in his eyes, her blood turned to ice. "Will? Oh, God, no! Please, no!"

Matt came around her desk and caught her hands. "Will's fine. Becky, it's…Nicolas."

A primal scream burst up from the deepest reaches of her soul. *"No! How?"*

He outlined what he knew, ending with, "Will's gone up there to find him."

Becky fought to make sense of what Matt was telling her. Will had gone up the mountain to find Nicolas? To the danger zone, too!

"How can he? He told me about the avalanche that nearly…killed him. He…said he has panic attacks just thinking of going up the mountain."

Matt nodded and said, "He loves Nick like a son. He'll bring him home to you."

WILL SLID OFF THE T-BAR, completing the last leg of his uphill journey to the avalanche zone. He traversed along the narrow ledge to the start of White Cloud Bowl.

The scene that confronted him chilled him to the core.

The entire expanse of the bowl was a mass of devastation. How would they ever find anyone in this mess?

Will and Craig kicked out of their skis and picked their way over chunks of ice, some bigger than a car, toward a group of rescuers. An avalanche-rescue dog barked excitedly as he helped them dig.

The other ski patroller was found minutes later and taken down the mountain in a rescue sled and evacuated by helicopter.

Another team was working its way upslope an arm's length apart, probing the snow as the probe-line leader called, "Down. Up and forward." And the searchers would probe once, between their feet, before moving forward.

Will breathed a sigh of relief at the sight of the coarse-probe search. A fine-probe search would mean body recovery.

He opened his probe and set to work. Sometimes the probe would hit ice or snow packed as hard as cement. Disappointed, he continued.

The only sounds were of the avalanche dogs barking occasionally as they patrolled in an organized search pattern, sniffing at the snow, then moving on.

Just below Will's position a ski pole was spotted. Soon after, a rescuer called, "Strike!" indicating his probe had hit something. Will raced to the spot and began digging a hole as wide as the depth of the probe's insertion into the snow. Other rescuers joined him. *Please let him be all right* was Will's mantra as he dug. *Please let it be Nick.*

Within minutes, a child was being hauled out.

Johnny Cooper! Will wanted to rail at the injustice of it. The kid wore the cockiest look and said, "Took you long enough."

Will grabbed the collar of his ski jacket. "Where's Nick?" he demanded.

"Hey! Git yer hands off me!" Johnny shouted. Then seeing the anger on Will's face, he broke into tears. "I want my mom!" he cried and implored the other rescuers. "He's hurtin' me!"

At the commotion, Lloyd Wilmott joined them. "Will—"

But Will knew Johnny—knew the tears were fake. "Show me where Nick was when the slope went," he yelled.

"I want my mom! I'm gonna sue you for hurtin' me!"

"Will!"

"*Dammit, Lloyd!* This kid is responsible for *all* this and I'm not letting him go down the mountain until we find every last kid here!"

"Will, you can't make him stay. He has a right to medical attention."

"Yeah, and if I don't git it, I'm gonna sue the whole ski patrol. You guys are useless!" Johnny cried.

Lloyd Wilmott brought his face close to the kid's and said, "My teams are risking their lives because of you, and you want to sue them?"

The kid sneered.

"Grateful little punk, aren't you?" Will asked in a mockingly sweet tone that changed to lethal when he shouted in a roar of adrenaline-fueled anger, *"Now, point to where everyone was or I'll personally take you down that mountain and, in front of everyone, hand you over to the police and tell them to lock you up and throw away the key!"*

"You can't do that," Johnny scoffed.

"Try me," Will growled. "I doubt anyone'll care once they hear you caused the slide and may have caused the death of others. At the very least, you're in trouble for a boundary violation. Now, where are the rest of them?"

He shrugged and said sulkily, "I don't remember."

Lloyd uttered an expletive and directed the other teams to search across the slope on a level similar to the one they'd found Johnny on.

Will stuck his face an inch from the kid's and demanded, *"Tell me!"*

He glared insolently back, then flung his hand casually around the slope as if he didn't give a damn about the devastation around him. "Over there."

The ski patroller who'd been rescued first and checked over

by a paramedic came over to join them. "This guy and his buddies were heading in this direction. You should be digging on the other side of him. The other kid was a lot farther up, doing a shallow traverse. He wasn't an experienced skier and he was calling out, but they ignored him. I think they were deliberately leaving him behind."

Directed by Lloyd, a team began digging in the area he'd indicated. They were joined by a dog team.

Johnny sneered as he watched them work. "He was so chickenshit he had to traverse the slope all the way across to the other side instead of skiin' down like us. If you ask me, *he's* the one who caused the avalanche."

With a growl of anger, Will released Johnny, grabbed his rescue backpack and headed uphill.

"Will! Be careful," Lloyd warned. "The slope up there is unstable."

But Will didn't care. He scrambled over huge boulders of ice and hard-packed snow, scanning the slope for any sign of ski clothing or equipment that might have been dislodged in the fall.

By the time his search team caught up with him, he'd already probed a small area.

BECKY PACED THE RESCUE headquarters set up for the relatives of victims. She hated that word. It implied there was no hope of bringing anyone out alive.

"Luke will be here soon, and Jack's on his way, too," Matt had told her as he tried to settle her in a seat to wait. But she was too impatient to sit.

"After what happened to Will, I can't imagine the courage it must've taken to go up there into the avalanche zone," she said.

Matt nodded grimly. "I'll come and get you if there's any news," he said before leaving to coordinate the contingent from the sheriff's department.

Becky looked toward the mountains. *My son and Will are up there somewhere.* To distract herself from thinking the worst, she concentrated on the organization of the rescue effort.

The base area of the mountain was abuzz. Snowmobiles zoomed back and forth, shuttling equipment, rescuers and their search dogs up the mountain. Mountain Rescue had erected a triage tent and the ski-school building was also being used. Firefighters, paramedics and law enforcement officers were everywhere.

The only people allowed past the police line were anxious parents collecting their children from the ski school and the families of those trapped. Becky wanted to give the parents of the boys who were with Johnny Cooper a piece of her mind about letting their sons hang around with such a thug. But she was too raw, too fragile, to deal with any of them right now.

"Becky!" Jack called as he strode up.

Her spirits lifted at seeing another friendly face. She clasped his hands. "I'm grateful you're here."

"They've found Johnny Cooper," Matt reported minutes later. "That's a positive sign—"

"But it's not Nicolas!" she cried, unable to keep the panic from her voice.

"Oh, honey," Jack soothed, rubbing her back in comforting strokes. "Will'll take good care of him."

Becky could only nod. Yes, Will would take care of her son, of that she was certain.

Sarah arrived with Luke. "Nick will be fine," Luke said. "Will's up there."

Sarah busied herself getting coffee for everyone. Edna Carmichael arrived with Miss Patterson, who immediately clasped Becky's hand. The small gesture managed to calm her like nothing else had. "Will adores your little boy. He'll bring him home to you," Miss Patterson murmured, her voice cracking with emotion.

Becky looked into her pale blue eyes and whispered, "Thank you."

Feeling guilty about keeping the older woman out in the cold, Becky drew her into the warmth of the shelter and sat and waited with her.

THE REST OF JOHNNY'S BUDDIES were pulled out within minutes. All were alive. All were mute with terror.

But there was still no sign of Nick.

Will was frantic. The chances of getting him out alive were slim to none, since it was now more than an hour since the slide. Then one of the rescuers let out a shout. His dog had found something. Several rescuers probed the area where the dog was digging so excitedly as Will scrambled toward them. With their probes, they established there was a body nine feet below them.

When a piece of Nick's jacket was removed with one of the probes, Will dug like a man possessed. "I'm coming, buddy," he muttered, moving three times as much snow as the others in a frantic race to uncover Nick and get him out of there alive.

A chunk of ice the size of a small car barred the way directly down, so they dug beneath it. As they neared the nine-foot mark, shovels were thrown aside and the rescuers dug the rest of the way with their hands.

Nick was buried beneath the huge block of ice, but the snow had held it back from crushing him. With a cry of elation, Will felt his hands touch something different in texture. It was the back of Nick's helmet. He sent up a silent prayer. The helmet would've protected Nick's head and kept him warmer.

Will pulled off his gloves and, heart racing, scratched away the snow, feeling for Nick's face to establish if he was conscious. His hand plunged into open space, confusing him until he realized the chunk of ice had created an air pocket.

Heart racing, he felt around while the other rescuers continued digging, mindful of the precarious state of the enormous ice cube hovering above them.

When a tiny hand closed over his, Will wanted to weep with joy. "He's alive!" he cried, desperate to get him out, but knowing they couldn't until he was checked by a paramedic.

"Can you hear me?" He prayed that first squeeze wasn't his imagination. He got two squeezes of his hand in return.

Tears filling his eyes, he said, "We're trying to get you out, champ. You…hold on there, okay? I'm going to stay with you the whole ti—"

Will was cut off by the blast of a whistle, warning that the slope was becoming more unstable. It was the signal for all rescuers to get off until it could be established that everything was safe.

"Will, I'm sorry," Lloyd said. "We have to go."

"I'm not leaving him. You go. But I'm not leaving until I get him out."

Will could hear hurried discussion from above, while he held Nick's hand tightly. If more of Nick's body had been freed, he'd have pulled him from the hole, but his legs were encased in hardened snow.

"Why don't you come with us, just for a bit," Lloyd urged as he crawled back into the hole. "It's probably a false alarm. We'll be back in no time."

"Then if it's a false alarm," Will said through his teeth, "there's no point in me leaving, is there? Now, go!"

Refusing to listen to any more entreaties, Will was soon left in silence as everyone deserted the slope until they were given the all clear.

MATT CAME BY TO REPORT. "They've found Nick! He's alive."

Becky and Miss Patterson burst into tears.

He laid a hand on her shoulder and said with a smile, "I told you Will would find him."

Speechless, Becky nodded through her tears.

WILL CONTINUED TALKING to Nick, reassuring him, as he worked with his free hand to try to clear the snow around the child's legs.

And then he heard an all-too-familiar sound.

Tearing the avalanche beacon off his jacket, Will threw it into the air pocket surrounding Nick. Moments later, he was wrenched from the hole by the churning snow and tumbled down the slope, completely at the mercy of nature's fury.

A GROUP OF RESCUERS came down the mountain. Exhausted, they were taking a break before heading back out again. If *they* were exhausted, how must Will be feeling? Becky wondered.

She was about to get coffee for Miss Patterson when a tremendous rumble echoed around the mountains.

She dropped the cup and raced outside, hoping to find Matt. She didn't care if she looked like a madwoman screaming at the top of her lungs. *"Matt!"*

He strode toward her, face grim.

She felt a knot of stomach-churning fear and could only manage one word. *"What?"*

"Will refused to leave the search area when they sounded the alarm to clear the slope. Now he's trapped, too."

Becky's knees liquefied and she sank to the snow. "Oh, God," she murmured. "Oh, God. Oh, God, no! Please, no," she begged.

"It's okay, Becky," Jack assured her as he and Luke helped her to her feet. "Will's wearing a beacon and as soon as they're confident the slope's stabilized they'll start searching again."

"Will's worked like a demon up there today," Matt said. "You should be proud of him."

"I am. I'm so very proud of him. For this…for everything."

"I'm sure he'll be here soon enough and you can tell him all that in person."

Becky gazed toward the mountains and prayed she'd get the chance.

THE SUN WAS SETTING when the whistle sounded, telling the rescuers they could resume the search. Every minute she'd waited had felt like an hour to Becky.

Television crews from Denver and the major news networks were broadcasting from their vans.

She heard one of the reporters saying to camera, "With every minute that passes, the hope of getting any more victims out alive decreases. Rescuers fear the last two victims are now dead."

Becky turned to Luke and said, "Get me out of here before I do something I might regret."

More rescuers came down to rest and change shifts. One told her about Will making contact with Nicolas. She found comfort in his words. Nicolas was alive, but buried deep, and Will had worked furiously to free him. "We couldn't drag him away from there, Judge McBride," he said. "When I got to the safety zone, I looked back and saw Will throw his avalanche beacon down the hole to your son." The man shook his head in wonder. "And then the slope went."

TEN MINUTES LATER, Matt gave her the news she'd been waiting for. "They've found Nick! Once they've checked the extent of his injuries—"

"Injuries?"

"Nothing too serious," he hastened to assure her. "But they won't move a patient until they're sure he's stable. Once that's done, he'll be down here in no time."

Heart in her throat, she asked, "And Will? He gave up his beacon to Nicolas."

Matt nodded and said, "Becky, there were a lot of rescuers watching when the slope went. They'd get a bearing on where Will might have ended up. It's not an exact science, but it's a help."

"Why can't you go up there and search?" she asked. "I know he'd want you there…in case…"

"Don't!" Matt warned, obviously guessing where her thoughts were heading. "I want to, believe me. But right now, I have to stay here. It's my job."

IT WAS NEARLY DARK when Matt came back with further news. "Nick's out and he's fine, apart from bruises and a dislocated shoulder."

Overwhelmed with relief, Becky and Sarah hugged each other. "Then he'll be here soon?" Sarah asked.

"I'm afraid not."

"*What?*" the two women asked at once.

"He's refusing to come down until they get Will out!"

Becky couldn't stop the laughter bubbling up inside her. "That damn stubborn pair!"

"They are, aren't they?" Matt agreed, unable to hide his smile.

"But won't Nicolas be cold?"

"I doubt he's worrying about his own comfort. The paramedics will have made sure he isn't hypothermic. He's in the heated cabin of one of the snow-grooming machines. They've been providing shelter for the rescuers when they need to take a break."

"Are…are they close to finding Will?"

He shook his head. "I wish I had the answer to that. When they do finally bring them down, they'll both be taken to the hospital."

"Hospital?" Becky wanted them safe at home with her.

"It's standard procedure," Matt explained. "They'll be thoroughly examined for internal injuries before they're released."

AS DAY TURNED TO NIGHT, every nerve in Becky's body wanted to scream as she realized there was probably no hope for Will now. She wanted to rail against the injustice of it. Will was a true hero. He'd sacrificed his life for another. For her son. She fought the grief threatening to overwhelm her.

"I can't stand this anymore," Matt said, his lips a tight line. "I'm going up there."

Becky's heart filled with hope. "The two most important people in the world to me are there, Matt. Please bring them back safely," she said, her voice choked with emotion and gratitude.

With a quick salute, he jumped onto a snowmobile and roared off.

She hugged herself against the cold. Matt would find Will and bring him back, she told herself. He wouldn't come down from the mountain until he did.

Jack joined her, linking his hand with hers. "I don't pray much these days, Becky, but if you'd like, I'll pray with you," he said.

She gazed into his deep blue eyes, so different from his brothers', and wondered again why he'd left the seminary.

She nodded, and they prayed silently together. *Please, God, keep Will safe.*

DARKNESS FELL, but the base area was flooded with light. To distract herself Becky put all her energy into seeing that Miss Patterson was comfortable. The elderly woman had refused to go home until she knew Will was safe. *Talk about stubborn!* Becky thought as she fetched more coffee.

"There's someone coming down!" Jack cried.

Becky raced outside. Sure enough, several snowmobiles, followed by a snow-grooming machine, were moving slowly down the mountain.

They were either taking care to transport patients carefully over the snow—or driving slowly out of respect for the... Becky shook her head to clear it of negative thoughts and approached the supervisor who'd taken over from Matt. "What's going on?"

He lifted a shoulder. "I don't know. Our communications cut out a few minutes ago and we haven't been able to restore them."

She forced herself to be patient, to wait and to hope. Sarah came to stand beside her, clasping her frozen hand as they waited for the slow procession to make its way down to them.

The wait seemed interminable as she peered through the darkness, trying to see who was on the lead snowmobile.

The radio crackled back to life and the operator gave a shout. "They're okay! They're both okay!"

Sarah and Becky turned to each other with a cry of triumph, hugging each other tightly as tears streamed down their cheeks.

"I have to go to him," Becky said. From the moment she'd heard they were coming down, she'd wanted to run up the slope to meet the small convoy. And now she did, surprised that her feet felt so light. The leading snowmobile broke from the ranks and charged toward her.

Matt was driving, his face split in a huge grin as he pulled up a few yards from her. His passenger eased himself off the seat behind him and stood unsteadily.

"Will!" she cried and closed the distance between them. He grunted as she flung her arms around him and held him close. "I'm so happy to see you!" she said and kissed his cold cheek.

"Where's Nicolas?" she asked, looking back at the slope.

"Telling the snow groomer how to drive his truck." He chuckled softly. "That kid has a lot of his mother in him!"

Becky grinned at his teasing remark and hugged him once more, just to be sure he was real. "I love you!" she cried.

He grunted again and brought her against him.

"Are you okay?" she asked, then drew back to look into his eyes. "You keep grunting."

"Broken ribs," he groaned and took in a ragged breath. In the light from the other rescue vehicles she could see that he was wincing with pain. "Say that again," he murmured.

"Are you all right?"

"The part before that."

"I love you."

His dark eyes bored into her. "Do you really?"

"Oh, yes!" she cried and kissed him. "Forever!"

He gave her a dimpled grin and said, "Then let's get our little guy and go home."

THEY ARRIVED BACK at Becky's house several hours later, after having their injuries attended to at the emergency room. Will had resisted going to the hospital, claiming he wanted to go home and maybe sleep for three days straight instead. But as soon as Becky heard the words *lung puncture* and *life threatening* when the paramedic mentioned the possible complications of broken ribs, she'd insisted he go to the hospital along with Nicolas.

Becky rode in one ambulance with Nicolas. Matt rode with Will in another. She fussed over her son and asked why he hadn't come down the mountain as soon as they got him out.

"I was sick with fear and worry, and all I wanted to do was hold you in my arms," she told him.

But Nicolas, with wisdom greater than his years, said, "If Will hadn't stayed, if he hadn't given me his beacon, they might never have found me again. I owe him my life, Mom. He stayed so I wouldn't be alone and I stayed so he wouldn't be alone, either. He's my buddy. And buddies stick together." Tears brightened his eyes and Becky had to wipe her cheeks for what seemed the hundredth time that day.

Will was a true hero. *Her* hero. She'd tell him that every day of their lives.

In spite of his dislocated shoulder, Nicolas had said he still wanted to sleep over at the ranch. The family had decided against attending Midnight Mass. After the day's events, both Will and Nicolas needed sleep. They'd go to mass the following day instead. The family had much to be thankful for this Christmas.

"He'll be fine, Becky," Sarah assured her. "He's been so excited about waking up on Christmas morning with Luke's girls." She covered her ears and laughed. "Can you imagine the noise?"

As he climbed into Luke's vehicle, he looked back and, ever the considerate child, asked, "Are you sure you won't be lonely, Mom? I could stay if you want."

Becky shook her head. "I'll be fine, sweetie. I'm going to wait up for Santa to come down the chimney."

His eyes opened wide, then narrowed briefly. "Grown-ups wait for Santa?"

"Sure they do," Will joined in, placing his hand on the back of Becky's neck.

Nicolas gazed at his hero. "See you tomorrow. Don't be late!"

Luke honked as he drove off and Will turned to her. "I hope I'm allowed to sleep over at your place."

She laughed and looped her arms around his neck, careful of his broken ribs. "I'm not sure *sleep* is what you had planned, but…okay," she teased, taking his hand to lead him up her front path.

Chapter Twenty-three

"I don't think I'll ever get enough of you," Becky murmured as she combed her fingers through Will's dark hair later that night. They'd made love—cautiously—swept up by the day's events and their insatiable need for each other.

A secret smile curved her lips. *Cooling it* hadn't stood a chance!

"Good," Will panted, trying to catch his breath. "Because I *know* I'll never get enough of you."

Emboldened, she pressed a kiss to his bandaged chest, then his throat, then his lips.

They kissed for long moments until Will pulled his mouth from hers and said, "We need to talk."

Becky expelled her breath with a whoosh. "That sounds ominous."

"Only if you think my asking you to marry me is ominous."

Becky couldn't help the smile that broke across her face. Unable to speak, she shook her head.

"No? You don't want to marry me?"

"Yes!"

"Yes, you don't want to marry me?"

"Oh, you annoying man!"

Will grinned, and she felt his teasing humor clear down to her toes. "What am I going to do with you, Will O'Malley?"

"I could suggest a number of things, several of them X-rated."

"Stop that!" she said, swatting his shoulder.

He lifted her hands and kissed each palm in turn, sending delicious shivers of anticipation pulsing through her.

"Will you marry me, Judge McBride? Can you see yourself spending the rest of your life in this town? Dealing with pesky pigs and sometimes annoying defendants? Having more children and living to a very old age? With me?"

"Yes! Yes, to all of it! Especially the growing old together part. I *really* like that."

"And the bit about having more children?"

"A whole passel of 'em!" she agreed, and Will laughed at her mountain slang.

"Do you think Nick will mind?"

"Are you kidding? He'd *love* brothers and sisters!"

"No, about us getting married."

"I can't believe you're even asking that. Nicolas *adores* you. Worships you. You're the best thing that's ever happened to my son—and to me."

He rewarded Becky with one of his smiles, then murmured in her ear, sending shivers of erotic pleasure vibrating through her, "Let's get started on that passel of kids right now."

AFTER ALLOWING WILL to sleep as long as he needed, Becky served him breakfast in bed. It was only coffee and croissants from the local bakery, but sharing them would become a tradition, she decided as she picked up a special Christmas Day edition of the paper and scanned the avalanche story.

Still too raw to deal with it, she turned the page and let out a whoop of delight. Will leaned over to see what had her so amused. Dugald, who was curled up at the foot of the bed, pricked up his ears.

She pointed to a photograph of Edna Carmichael and Frank Farquar announcing their engagement. It included a brief story of how they'd dated many years ago and recently—thanks to joint efforts to save an integral part of their town's history—rekindled their love. It closed with a statement that Louella had given her snort of approval to the match.

"Only in Spruce Lake!" Becky said. "What a wonderful, uplifting story."

"We could have a double wedding. I'm sure Lou would love to be our bridesmaid."

"Don't even think about it!" She laughed, then said, "We should get dressed. The children will be waiting for us so they can open their gifts."

As if on cue, the phone rang.

"Mom?" Nicolas said, bringing Becky back to earth. "Where *are* you? We want to open our gifts. And you wouldn't believe it—Santa *knew* I was sleeping over at Sasha's. He's left all my presents here!"

Becky smiled at the excitement in his voice. "I told you Santa's magical, sweetie. I'm getting dressed now. See you soon. Oh, and Merry Christmas!"

She hung up the phone and said, "He's very impressed that Santa knew where he was staying last night."

Will grinned. "Santa will know where he's staying for the rest of his life, if I have anything to say about it."

Sudden tears brimmed in Becky's eyes.

Will wrapped his arms around her, asking, "Did I say something wrong?"

She placed her hand over his strongly beating heart and said, "No, you said everything right." She dabbed at her eyes with a tissue. "It's been a very emotional twenty-four hours for me. I don't know what I would have done if I'd lost either of you in the aval—"

Her words were interrupted by Will kissing her. When he finally drew away, he whispered, "Let's not talk about it again, okay? At least not for a long, long time."

She nodded, stroking his cheek. "I love you, Will, and I don't ever want to be parted from you."

"Ditto!" He kissed the tip of her nose. "We'd better get moving. Miss Patterson will be waiting for her ride. Mom invited her to spend Christmas with us."

“THERE YOU ARE!” four children chimed as they entered the living room at Two Elk.

“We’ve been waiting forever ’n’ ever,” Celeste told her uncle, a frown creasing her brow.

He hoisted her onto his hip, wincing at the effort. “Merry Christmas, cupcake,” he said and nuzzled her neck, causing her to burst into squeals of laughter.

When he set her back on her feet, his other nieces and Nick demanded equal attention, and from then on, the morning was an endless round of gift opening and exclamations of surprise.

WHEN THE LAST GIFT had been opened—a saddle for Daisy—Will brought Becky to stand beside the Christmas tree with him.

He cleared his throat and said, “I have an announcement to make.”

Becky smiled as eleven pairs of eyes widened.

“This wonderful woman—” he raised Becky’s hand to his lips “—has consented to marry me—”

“Hallelujah!” Matt cried and leaped to his feet. He grabbed Becky in a bear hug. “Welcome to the family, Becky,” he said, then turned to Will and shook his hand, saying, “It’s about time, little brother!”

“Hey! We’ve only known each other a few weeks!” Will protested with a laugh.

“More than long enough!” his father yelled above the commotion of screaming children as he came to offer his congratulations.

Surrounded by *family,* Becky dabbed at her eyes and hugged Nicolas to her as he said, “Mom, this is the best Christmas present in the world!”

Epilogue

The next December...

"My turn now!" Nicolas said, reaching for his baby sister.

With an indulgent smile, Becky handed four-week-old Lily Emma O'Malley over to him. He settled her against him and cooed at her. She offered him a toothless, deep-dimpled grin.

"Do you think she knows I'm her big brother?" he asked, his eyes imploring Becky for an affirmative answer.

"How could she not, buddy?" Will said as he sat on the sofa beside his adopted son. "You've done nothing but boss her around since she got here."

Nicolas chuckled and tickled Lily under her chin, something he'd discovered was guaranteed to have her gurgling with pleasure.

Becky's heart overflowed with love and happiness as the two men in her life gazed in wonder at the most recent addition to their family.

How things have changed in the past year! she thought. It was a year to the day since she'd first met Will.

They were married at the end of January and she'd become pregnant almost immediately. Job sharing with Judge Stevens had turned out even better than Becky had hoped, and now that she was on maternity leave, another young judge had come to live in Spruce Lake. Would Judge Jenny Chesterfield also find love in this quirky, wonderful town?

The old buildings on Main Street were gradually being restored, attracting a lot of publicity and even awards for their sensitive renovation. Frank had moved back to town and married Edna Carmichael. She still ran her florist shop on Main Street but would soon relocate the business to new premises a short walk from Frank's and her restored Victorian home. They'd moved in before Thanksgiving, and the housewarming was a huge event, attended, it seemed, by half the town.

Frank, of course, needed an elegant home to call his own since he'd been elected mayor of Spruce Lake by an overwhelming majority.

Miss Patterson still lived in town, but next summer intended to move to the new independent-living units being constructed at the Twilight Years. Will popped in to visit her several times a week and she still baked him chocolate chip cookies.

Matt had been elected county sheriff. Will, true to his promise, had been both Matt's campaign manager and project manager of the buildings' restoration. The brothers had forged an even closer bond. They still bickered occasionally, but Matt had learned to take less umbrage at Will's teasing and Will had found a new respect for his older brother.

Nicolas was thriving. He loved being part of the O'Malley clan. When school had resumed in January, he'd entered the same grade as Sasha. Now that they were cousins, they were more inseparable than ever, and Nicolas had made other friends at school, too. He'd competed in his first swim meet last summer. Although he'd come last in the race, the memory of the standing ovation he'd received from the crowd still brought tears to Becky's eyes.

Sarah was right; Nicolas didn't need to be intellectually challenged all the time. He'd learned far more about life by hanging out with Will than he would have if he'd attended a school for gifted kids. And he was happy. Unbelievably happy.

For the moment, they were still living in her rented Victorian in town, but come summer they'd be moving into the beautiful home Jack was building for them on Will's land. She smiled at that. The ranchettes were a runaway success and she was delighted that Matt had purchased the lot next door—at a heavily discounted price—and would be their neighbor sometime in the future.

And Will had started skiing again. He and Matt had a regular ski date each week. He'd promised to teach Becky, once she felt ready to give it a try. She was sure that eventually she'd be able to face going up the mountains that had nearly claimed Nicolas's and Will's lives—but not just yet.

"Can we go buy our tree now?" Nicolas asked.

"It's too cold to take Lily out, sweetie," she said.

"I was asking Dad, Mom!" Nicolas, said, sounding exasperated.

Becky grinned. She still hadn't gotten used to Nicolas asking Will's permission for anything. For so long, it had been just the two of them.

"You don't need me to help choose the tree?" she asked, pretending hurt at being excluded.

Will hugged her. "Choosing Christmas trees is best left to men. Trust me on this." He pressed her down to sit on the sofa. Nicolas handed Lily to her.

"We'll bring you back some ice cream, okay?" he offered and went to put on warmer clothes.

Dugald lifted his head at the prospect of a walk. After they decided it might be too cold out for him, too, he returned to his doggie dreams.

Will bent to nuzzle Lily's cheek and kiss Becky. He was about to pull away but she clutched his shirtfront and kept him there.

She kissed him with all the love in her heart, then whispered in his ear, "Hurry home. And don't you *dare* buy a bigger tree than last year!"

* * * * *

"Don't die on me. Come on, Zel. You know how much I love you, girl. You're all I've got. Don't do this to me here. Not *now*."

But Zelda had quit on him, and Zach Beaudry had no one to blame but himself. He'd taken his sweet time hitting the road, and then miscalculated a shortcut. For all he knew he was a hundred miles from gas. But even if they were sitting next to a pump, the ten dollars he had in his pocket wouldn't get him out of South Dakota, which was not where he wanted to be right now. Not even his beloved pickup truck, Zelda, could get him much of anywhere on fumes. He was sitting out in the cold in the middle of nowhere. And getting colder.

He shifted the pickup into Neutral and pulled hard on the steering wheel, using the downhill slope to get her off the blacktop and into the roadside grass, where she shuddered to a standstill. He stroked the padded dash. "You'll be safe here."

But Zach would not. It was getting dark, and it was already too damn cold for his cowboy ass. Zach's battered body was a barometer, and he was feeling South Dakota, big time. He'd have given his right arm to be climbing into a hotel hot tub instead of a brutal blast of north wind. The right was his free arm anyway. Damn thing had lost altitude, touched some part of the bull and caused him a scoreless ride last time out.

It wasn't scoring him a ride this night, either. A carload of teenagers whizzed by, topping off the insult by laying on the horn as they passed him. It was at least twenty minutes before another vehicle came along. He stepped out and waved both arms this time, damn near getting himself killed. Whatever happened to *do unto others?* In places like this, decent people didn't leave each other stranded in the cold.

His face was feeling stiff, and he figured he'd better start walking before his toes went numb. He struck out for a distant yard light, the only sign of human habitation in sight. He couldn't tell how distant, but he knew he'd be hurting by the time he got there, and he was counting on some kindly old man to be answering the door. No shame among the lame.

It wasn't like Zach was fresh off the operating table—it had been a few months since his last round of repairs—but he hadn't given himself enough time. He'd lopped a couple of weeks off the near end of the doc's estimated recovery time, rigged up a brace, done some heavy-duty taping and climbed onto another bull. Hung in there for five seconds—four seconds past feeling the pop in his hip and three seconds short of the buzzer.

He could still feel the pain shooting down his leg with every step. Only this time he had to pick the damn thing up, swing it forward and drop it down again on his own.

Pride be damned, he just hoped *somebody* would be answering the door at the end of the road. The light in the front window was a good sign.

The four steps to the covered porch might as well have been four hundred, and he was looking to climb them with a lead weight chained to his left leg. His eyes were just as screwed up as his hip. Big black spots danced around with tiny red flashers, and he couldn't tell what was real and what wasn't. He stumbled over some shrubbery, steadied himself on the porch railing and peered between vertical slats.

There in the front window stood a spruce tree with a silver star affixed to the top. Zach was pretty sure the red sparks were all in his head, but the white lights twinkling by the hundreds throughout the huge tree, those were real. He wasn't too sure about the woman hanging the shiny balls. Most of her hair was

:aught up on her head and fastened in a curly clump, but the light :aptured by the escaped bits crowned her with a golden halo. Her ace was a soft shadow, her body a willowy silhouette beneath ı long white gown. If this was where the mind ran off to when :old started shutting down the rest of the body, then Zach's final vorldly thought was, *This ain't such a bad way to go.*

If she would just turn to the window, he could die looking nto the eyes of a Christmas angel.

* * * * *

Could this woman from Zach's past
get the lonesome cowboy to come in
from the cold...for good?
Look for
ONE COWBOY, ONE CHRISTMAS
by Kathleen Eagle
Available December 2009
from Silhouette Special Edition®

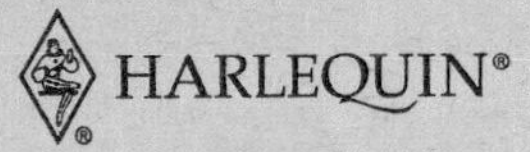

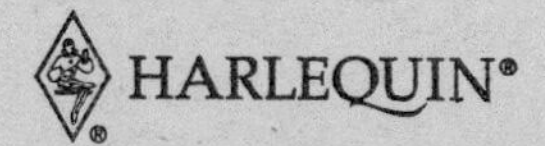

American★Romance®

COMING NEXT MONTH

Available December 8, 2009

#1285 THE WRANGLER by Pamela Britton

Men Made in America

For as long as she can remember, Samantha Davies has dreamed of Montana's legendary Baer Mountain mustangs. She has to see for herself if there's truth behind the legend...before she loses her sight forever. And nothing, not even the devil-handsome wrangler Clint McAlister—who has every reason to distrust Samantha's intentions—is going to stand in her way. Because time is running out.

#1286 A MOMMY FOR CHRISTMAS by Cathy Gillen Thacker

The Lone Star Dads Club

With four preschoolers between them, neighbors and single parents Travis Carson and Holly Baxter don't know what they'd do without each other. And they don't want to find out! Everything changes when Travis's little girls ask Santa for a mommy for Christmas. Their entire Texas town gets in on the hunt for an available mom…who happens to live right next door.

#1287 HER CHRISTMAS WISH by Cindi Myers

The only thing Alina Allinova wants for Christmas is to stay in the U.S.—oh, and Eric Sepulveda. They're having a fairy-tale romance, yet the possibility of sharing a happily-ever-after seems far away, with her visa expiring soon. Still, her fingers are crossed that come Christmas morning she'll get her wish and find him under her tree!

#1288 A COWBOY CHRISTMAS by Marin Thomas

2 stories in 1!

The holidays are a rough time for widower Logan Taylor and single dad Fletcher McFadden—neither hunky cowboy has been lucky in love. But Christmas *is* the season of miracles! Logan meets his match in "A Christmas Baby," while Fletcher gets a second chance at love in "Marry Me, Cowboy." This year both cowboys are on Santa's Nice list!

www.eHarlequin.com

HARCNMBPA1109